I Want Your Hex

CRESCENT MOON MYSTERY #2

TARA LUSH

COVER DESIGN
LOU HARPER/ COVER AFFAIRS

EDITED BY
THE AUTHOR BUDDY

One

With a small nudge of my index finger, I shifted the plastic tiara atop the head of the five-foot-tall taxidermied alligator an inch to the left. The gator stood on its hind legs, its stubby forearms extended as though it were reaching for a drink.

"Liz?" I called out to my friend.

"Amelia?"

"What did my aunt call this gator, anyway? Does it have a name?" In the weeks since my father's sister died and left me a three-story Queen Anne Victorian in a small Florida town, some large and small details had eluded me. Mostly because I'd been busy playing matchmaker to a wayward spirit that had plagued the place. He was living *his* best life with his sweetheart in the afterlife now, so I was free to go about my own life.

"George," Liz squeaked in a girlish voice that sounded far younger than her fifty years. "His name is George."

The phone trilled, and she snatched it up on the first ring while simultaneously turning the volume down on the Bluetooth speaker. We'd been listening to Elle King croon with sass.

"Crescent Moon Inn, how can I help y'all? No, this is Liz

Lopez. Amelia Matthews is the new owner. She's the niece of the previous owner, who passed. Yes, thank you for your condolences. Oh, you want to make a reservation? I can help."

I nudged the tiara another millimeter. Then I wielded my glue gun, squirting a dab on the gator's rough head to adhere the tiara to the creature. Hmm. *Sparkly.*

I tilted my head to admire my handiwork. I'd bought an entire pack of the plastic tiaras, thinking the bachelorettes that had booked the inn for the weekend might want them as party favors. Putting one on the gator was the best decision I'd made all day.

"Georgina," I whispered. I was aiming for more kitschy and less serial killer creepy here in the inn's lobby. "Perfect."

For a solid half-day, I'd pondered whether to give the weird, long-dead creature away. But no, my aunt had bought it at an auction, one where she'd also French-kissed the auctioneer. I'd found this out in part by talking with the mailman, who'd been at the auction that evening.

Needless to say, I couldn't get rid of it after learning that particular story. I placed my palm on the creature's scaly body and closed my eyes. My hand, then arm, tingled, and a scene played out in my mind. It was vivid as a movie.

Aunt Shirley jumped up, hands above her head in triumph. She was in the middle of a packed room and almost toppled over the chair. "It's mine? It's really mine?"

"The life-sized, stand-up gator — a real one, I might add, dead, not alive — is sold to Shirley Hall, the woman in the flower-print caftan," a male voice boomed. "And that's all for tonight's auction."

I felt a rush of adrenaline as my aunt walked quickly to the front of the room, in the opposite direction of the crowd. Her colorful muumuu billowed behind her. The auctioneer, a man with a handlebar moustache and an impressive head of thick, gray hair, grinned. "Congratulations, Shirley. That thing's going to look great in the hotel."

"Come here, you sexy hunk," she cried.

The auctioneer reached for her, kissing her hand. Then her wrist. Then up her arm, Gomez Addams-style.

"What the duck?" I whispered in the vision. There had been a time in my life where I swore like a long-haul trucker. When I'd typed a text to my ex-husband, the stupid phone always autocorrected my (formerly) favorite word to *duck*. Now I used that instead whenever I needed emphasis. Or expressed surprise.

I snatched my hand away and the scene faded. That was another shock since arriving in Cypress Grove a few weeks ago: I possessed the power of psychometry. By touching items, I could see, and sometimes feel, things from the past. Including emotions.

It was proving to be a rather wonky superpower. On the upside, it helped me solve a cold-case murder here at the hotel. On the downside, I was starting to realize I needed to be mindful of what I touched and where. It felt wrong to peer into my aunt's most private moments, like kissing the auctioneer.

Lines had to be drawn *somewhere*.

The power was strongest here at the hotel, although I'd notice the ability was ramping up elsewhere in town, too. I'd been inundated with memories and emotions while going through my aunt's things, so much so that I took to wearing latex gloves. Other items, everyday things such as pens and computers and the mail, didn't seem to carry energy in them. Or perhaps nothing interesting had occurred involving those items.

Prior to coming to Cypress Grove, I'd never given much thought about psychic powers or new age woo woo stuff. I'd done a bit of yoga, but if I was asked to name five chakras, I'd have guessed nausea, heartburn, indigestion, upset stomach and diarrhea.

That ignorance was in the past, however. With the help of some new friends who were experts in all things telepathic and psychic here in town, I'd learned that I could also control my power with my mind. It wasn't necessary to feel and experience everything. It was all about focus.

"Amelia? Amelia!"

The sound of a phone handset connecting with the cradle and Liz's voice ripped me out of my vision.

"Yeah? Sorry, I was communing with Georgina the gator. What's up?"

"That was another guest. They've booked the entire second week of November."

I walked over to the desk, which was an old wooden thing. It was one of the few pieces I wanted to replace soon, mostly because it was dark and imposing. So was the rest of the room, but I was slowly redecorating with more whimsy and less dank. Already I'd gotten new, gauzy pink curtains and painted the walls a pale pink.

Addams Family meets Hello Kitty, I'd explained to my new friends here in town.

"Really? That's the third weeklong booking today. What's going on?" I chewed on my lip as I stood next to Liz, staring at the reservation screen.

"Luck? The Universe? Rumors about the hotel being haunted? That's probably it. Who knows?" Liz shrugged. "Whatever it is, you're going to be busy. You might want to consider hiring another person."

I tapped on the keyboard, bringing up the calendar view. "You're probably right, but I don't feel comfortable spending that kind of money. I think Jimbo and I will be able to handle things. Right?"

Jimbo had been my aunt's lone employee. He was out running errands today, buying a case of champagne for the bachelorette party scheduled to arrive at any moment.

I smiled at Liz. "Thank you for helping me today. I know it's not something you can do again. I feel terrible that you're neglecting your own business."

Liz was the owner of a popular new age shop in town, but had offered to assist today with my first official hotel guests. We figured we'd make a party of it, and both of us wore witchy-looking black dresses.

She waved me away. "Nonsense. I put a sign on the door telling people they could find me here, or call. There's never an emergency on a Thursday in October. People are too excited about Halloween."

"They sure are," I murmured, looking through all of the reservations that had come in.

Cypress Grove was a popular tourist spot in Florida. Sure, it wasn't Disney, but for folks who were looking for a psychic, medium, astrologer, reiki healer, aura cleansing, spiritual masseuse, or tarot card reader, it was like a theme park and South Beach all rolled into one. Decades ago, the town had been dubbed "The Psychic Capital of the World" by The New York Times because of all the energy workers who had visited and stayed. The nickname stuck, and now the town embraced all things New Age.

This had all come as a shock when I first arrived a few weeks ago. The town's psychic history, my newfound ability, the legacy of my late aunt's historic hotel. It was all so wonderfully weird.

"Want to go over the weekend's events again?" Liz asked. She knew I was nervous. I had no background in hotel hospitality, unless you counted the years I owned a cookie delivery service in California.

"Sure." I reached for my notepad. "Okay, tonight's the haunted swamp walk. Oliver's meeting us there at seven with his head full of ghost stories. The actors will be there, too. Hopefully."

I held up my hand and crossed my fingers.

"You were so lucky that came together in a flash."

I shot her a relieved look. "No kidding. That other inn owner was a lifesaver. I meant to tell you about that. I've been so busy—"

"What?" Liz tilted her head. "What inn owner? There's only one other B&B in town."

"Didn't I tell you? When I was looking around for a ghost walk for the bachelorette party, I went to the coffee shop."

"Witches Brew or Ice Ice Baby?"

"Ice Ice Baby. I can't get enough of their caramel apple iced coffee."

She groaned pleasurably. "Super tasty."

It was the best coffee I'd had in years. "I went in and was chatting with the baristas about who organizes ghost walks in town when a woman came up to me. In her thirties, name's Helena. Cute. Adorable. Was dressed in head-to-toe black. Although, that might not narrow it down."

Liz's face contorted in horror. "Helena Blackwood? Of the Lakeview Inn?"

I pointed. "Yeah, that's her. Why the shocked expression?"

Her mouth opened and closed a few times. "How do I say this? Uh. Helena is, um..."

My eyes widened as I waited for her to finish the sentence.

"She's... she disliked your aunt. Hated her. Was the only one in town who did. She and I have also had run-ins."

"Really?" I reared back. Liz was the sunniest, most

outgoing person I'd met in decades. It was difficult to believe anyone would have a beef with her. "Helena? She's so cute and unassuming. Super complimentary and pleasant. Said she was sorry to hear of Shirley's passing and that she meant to stop by and meet me soon. Asked to get together for lunch."

Liz winced. "Yeah, if you want her to poison you."

"Oh, come on. She was so nice. And I think I can take her if she tries to attack me." I took a boxing stance with my fists in the air, then laughed. "She has a group of bachelorettes at her place this weekend, too. Apparently, October's the time for that sort of thing, for fall brides. Anyway, she'd organized a haunted swamp walk, and said it would be no problem if my guests tagged along. I accepted and obviously offered cash for her trouble. It solved so many problems for me."

"I dunno about this," Liz muttered. "But I shouldn't poison the well with my own biases, I guess. I'll be nice."

"Why does she dislike you?"

Liz took a deep breath. "Helena is convinced she has psychic abilities. She reads tarot cards and claims she can predict the future."

I chuckled. "What's the problem with that? Sounds like almost everyone in town."

"I think she's full of B.S. A couple of years ago, she did a reading for me. She looked at me, all serious, and said she sensed that I was entering a 'great transition' and that I needed to 'embrace the shift.' She was talking about menopause! But I'd already gone through the change."

I snorted aloud. "Oops! Are you serious?"

"She went on and on about how I needed to 'navigate the cosmic tides' and 'balance my internal fire.' Naturally, I thought it was hilarious. I mean, menopause is a 'great transition,' but it seemed so simple and even hokey to say it aloud. She had all the hallmarks of someone who is a psychic scammer. I expected something more meaningful! Of course, I let my inner comic out and started cracking jokes. I asked if my hot flashes were going to get me mistaken for a fire-wielding witch and if I'd levitate during night sweats."

"And she didn't take it well?"

Liz shook her head, grinning. "Oh, you have no idea. She got so offended. Said I was mocking 'sacred energies' and that I should prepare for 'cosmic retribution.' Since then, she's avoided me like the plague and bad-mouthed me to anyone who'd listen. The fact that I was close to your aunt sealed the deal."

I laughed so hard my sides hurt. "Cosmic retribution? What did she think was going to happen? Your estrogen levels were going to go rogue and create a psychic imbalance?"

"Who knows? She's a character, that's for sure. With her 'psychic powers,' she might predict your 'great transition' into life as the new owner of a bed-and-breakfast in a quirky small town. Seriously." Liz's smile faded. "There are rumors of her dabbling in black magic. Be careful around her, okay?"

"I have no idea what that means and don't want to know," I said, only a little spooked that I was about to go on a haunted swamp walk with someone who was allegedly involved in 'black magic,' whatever that was. "But why would she hate Shirley? And if she had a beef with the Crescent Moon Inn, why invite me and my guests? She was thrilled when I told her Oliver could come and tell ghost stories."

Liz snorted. "I'm sure she was thrilled about that. She's had pants feelings for him for years."

"Huh? Pants what?"

Liz's chuckle was back, and it made me laugh, too. "I learned that phrase from my daughter. Aren't Gen Z kids inventive with their phrases? It means lusting after someone. Pants feelings."

My own college-age daughter was always trying to explain new lingo to me, and usually failed. "I'll have to try that on my kid. She'll probably roll her eyes."

I told Liz how Helena had called in a favor to a troupe of performers who worked at the theme parks in Orlando. A dozen of them were going to dress up as spooky creatures and surprise us on the swamp walk, while Oliver Everhart — a charmingly handsome local professor and author — had agreed to tell ghost stories.

I'd arranged that part, partially because yes, apparently like every other woman in town, I harbored a little crush on Oliver. But I also enjoyed a good spooky story. Something told me that Halloween ghost tales were on another level here in Cypress Grove.

"You need to be real careful, hon," Liz said in an exaggerated southern accent. She was great with different voices, switching easily between down-home Old Florida and her Cuban grandma's Spanish lilt. "Hey, have you heard from Jimbo or Sage?"

"No, can't say that I have." We'd sent Jimbo out an hour ago for the champagne, and Sage — Oliver's sister and a witch in training — was supposed to come over in costume to greet the bridesmaids. While I had considered dressing up, I figured I had enough to worry about.

I wanted to ask Liz about Helena's relationship with my late aunt, but as if on cue, the front door flew open, accompanied by two excited voices.

"This is some pricey champagne, pardner. I would've gotten something a bit more economically friendly. Let's face it, once you've finished one bottle, you don't know or care about the quality of the second."

That was Sage, and her raspy voice cut through the lobby. She boomed a hello and was carrying a giant orchid plant.

She was followed closely by Jimbo, who was toting a box with the words VEUVE CLIQUOT on the side. They looked like total opposites. She was in a denim dress and cowboy boots, while he looked like...

Florida Man.

Jimbo sported a mullet, a trucker cap, jeans, flip-flops, and a T-shirt branded with a beer can.

"The guests paid for this kind specifically," he said to Sage, then turned to me. "Where do you want this, Miss Amelia?"

I drummed my fingers on the desk. "I cleaned out a shelf in the apartment fridge. That's as good a place as any. Let's get those bottles chilled."

My aunt had lived in a small apartment on the first floor of the inn. It was the perfect size for me — I was single, with only my cat Freddie Purrcury to care for. But I wasn't ready to move here yet. There was the issue of my aunt's things, which I wasn't emotionally prepared to sort through.

Going through personal belongings was fraught with even more difficulty when one had a psychic ability.

Freddie and I were staying in a temporary spot, a garage studio on Oliver's property. Sage lived in the backyard in a tiny house, and over the past weeks, the three of us had become quite chummy. Still, I planned to stay the weekend in the apartment while the women were here, so I'd toted Freddie along.

He was ensconced in the apartment, probably snoozing.

"Sounds good," Jimbo said, loping out of the room. "Nobody likes warm bubby."

"I'm gonna put on my costume," Sage declared. "Can I use the facilities?"

I studied her for a beat. Something was odd. Parts of her face had a weird blue hue. "Sure, but... are you okay?"

"Yeah. Why?"

Taking a few steps closer while squinting, I replied, "You look blue."

"I'm in a great mood!" She grinned. "Can't wait to put on my costume."

"I didn't mean emotionally. Blue as in, the color. Your face is bluish-purple. There's a weird blue streak on your forehead. And your hands are the same color." I glanced down. Her nails were a strange purple-azure color. "Or is that part of your costume?"

"Are you taking too much colloidal silver again, Sage?" Liz looked up, concerned, then muttered, "Where are my reading glasses?"

They were on her head. I pointed to my own skull.

"Oh, right," she said.

"I'm not taking anything," Sage said defensively, then blew out a sigh. "Sorry. I discovered five gray hairs and I used purple shampoo for the first time. It got everywhere and I think I left it on too long, dangit."

"Oh, Sage." I moved closer to her. She looked so sad that I couldn't help but fold her into a hug. Sage was a little younger than Liz, Oliver, and me. At forty-two, she was the baby of my new friend group. "That's a tough day, finding the first gray hair."

Liz came over. "Gray is in now, you know. Embrace the silver."

She shook her mop of salt-and-pepper curls and they bounced like a shampoo commercial.

"I thought the purple stuff would make my silver sparkle," Sage whispered. "It got all over me and now I look like a danged extra in the Blue Man Group. Also..."

"What?"

Her face had twisted into a grimace. "Oliver's going to be

upset. I think I permanently stained the walls and the grout in the guest bathroom."

"Oh dear," I said. "I'm sure he won't mind."

It was difficult to imagine kind, sweet, handsome Oliver getting upset at something so silly. But he wasn't my brother, and since I had a brother of my own, I was aware of how annoying siblings could be. Yeah, if Mike stained my shower, I'd make him clean it. Then get him to buy me a margarita.

"Guess I'm going to get into costume. At least the blue will look good with that," Sage said.

"You know where the downstairs bathroom is, right?" There was a lavatory with ornate brass fixtures and a stuffed crow above the toilet near the library. It would have been a dream commode for Edgar Allen Poe, a favorite of my aunt's.

"Sure do. Oh, and here." She set the beautiful orange orchid on the desk. It was in a ceramic pot decorated with cute cartoon ghosts. "This is Jimbo's. Well, it's yours. I just carried it in. He wanted you to have it."

She power-walked outside, probably to grab her bag. Liz and I admired the gorgeous flowers.

"I wonder where he got this," she mused. "These can be difficult to grow."

"I've never kept one alive. Then again, I have a black thumb. Not a green one."

She fiddled with the Bluetooth speaker and it began playing a song from Rocky Horror. Oliver and I had spent last night carefully curating tonight's playlist of spooky songs.

Liz and I made small talk while I nervously tidied up. This felt like the first day of school. I'd even bought a new dress for the occasion: a cute, black frock with a full skirt, and emblazoned with cute orange ghosts.

"Do you think it's going to get easier?" I asked, peeking

behind a bust of a grim-looking fellow. A dust bunny sat there, ripe for the taking. I reached for my feather duster.

"What?" Liz responded.

"Waiting for guests. Getting ready for guests. Greeting guests. I'm more excited than a girl on prom night." I carefully dusted behind the carved marble man. "Who is this guy, anyway?"

"Oh, that's Dr. John Gorrie. He's a Florida man who invented air conditioning. And yes, you'll eventually relax and be excited about new guests. Your aunt sure was."

I fluttered Dr. Gorrie's face with the duster. He deserved sainthood, as far as I was concerned. "I just want everything to be—"

Before I could finish my sentence, the front door eased open. A woman in a comically large straw beach hat peeked in.

"Hello? Anyone here? Oh, you're here! Ladies? Let's go!"

The door swung fully open. Three women, all toting suitcases, backpacks, shopping bags, purses, garment bags, and coolers, tumbled in. Liz and I watched in awe as they and their luggage all found their way into the middle of the lobby.

One of the women, a blonde in jeans, black spike heels, and a Barbie pink T-shirt that said, MATRON OF HONOR, stepped out of the fray.

"Hi, I'm Lauren Turner. I'm the one who emailed y'all and organized everything. This here's the bride." She reached for the woman in the hat, who giggled and stepped forward. "Her name's Bella Copperfield. And this is one of the bridesmaids, Megan McCall."

She flicked her hand in the other woman's direction. Megan didn't smile. She only raised a hand in a wave. I couldn't tell if she was shy or didn't want to be here. I had a vague recollection from one of the email chains for their reservation that Megan was someone's cousin. The bride's, perhaps.

"We have another bridesmaid coming. Nia Jones. She has to work late and will meet us here later," Bella said apologetically.

Lauren rolled her eyes. "Nia's always late."

I introduced myself and Liz. "You all have the honor of being my first guests. I recently took over ownership of the Crescent Moon, and I..." My voice trailed off because none of the three women were listening. They were talking amongst themselves.

"No, I think we should open the sangria. We'll save the champagne for later," Lauren whined.

"But the champagne is chilled. Megan, what do you think?" Bella asked the woman.

Megan shrugged and I thought I saw a subtle eye roll. Nope, she did not want to be here. I wondered what their story was, and how they all fit together. Megan was short, curvy, and had a mop of dark, curly hair. Oddly, she kind of resembled Liz. Enough that I'd believe they were mother and daughter.

"Don't ask her, she'll drink anything," Lauren said in a snotty tone.

Yikes. When I owned the cookie delivery company, I'd seen my share of difficult brides. Bella had shades of bridezilla, which added an extra dimension to my nerves. With women like that, nothing was ever good enough.

Liz began passing out the plastic tiaras. Bella refused hers. "Brought my own," she cried, pulling out something larger, gaudier, and not plastic. She replaced her hat with the tiara.

Hoping to get everyone's attention so they could check in, get their keys, and drink calmly upstairs, I raised my hand. "Hey, everyone. I'd like to get you all squared away with paperwork and stuff. The champagne—"

"The champagne is here!" Sage burst into the room, wearing a royal blue velvet witch costume, an enormous matching hat, and black cowboy boots with rhinestones. Black lace and taffeta seemed to drip off her like Spanish moss.

She held two bottles of bubbly in both hands. Her lips were a dark blue-black and the purple streaks on her face blended perfectly. "Welcome to the Crescent Moon Inn!"

The women cheered, then whooped louder when they spotted Jimbo following close behind Sage. He was holding a tray of flutes filled with pink champagne — and each glass held a little spider ring. There was also a pile of snickerdoodle cookies on a plate that I'd whipped up a few hours ago. Sweet snickerdoodles and dry bubbly paired nicely, I'd discovered.

The three women circled, practically attacking him for the drinks and snacks.

Jimbo didn't seem to mind because he wore a giant smile. "Easy now, ladies."

"Who's ready for a killer bachelorette weekend?" Sage cried.

Two

I slowed the hotel's van to a stop about ten feet from a group of people who were standing near a nature center and a trailhead. We were at the Marigold Wentworth Cypress Boardwalk Trail, a local park that apparently had miles of wooden walkways winding over and through a swamp.

I hadn't been here yet because not only had I been busy since arriving in town, but the idea seemed a little creepy. I knew very little about Florida, but I suspected this was one of the places where gators, snakes, and other creepy crawlies lived.

Although, tonight in the twilight, the place seemed innocuous and pleasant. Kids played on a nearby playground, while parents watched and chatted.

"Who is that hot daddy?" Lauren said while flipping her long, glossy blonde hair behind her. She pointed at a tall, raven-haired man with black-rimmed glasses and a slightly hipster, button-down linen shirt. He was standing next to Sage, who drove over with Jimbo.

"That's Oliver Everhart. He'll be doing the ghost stories tonight."

Lauren, who was sitting in the passenger seat, whipped around. "Did you hear that? We've got a hot, spooky storyteller! Woot!"

She and Bella high fived.

"Maybe you'll get lucky tonight," Bella said to Lauren, who cackled.

For the first time, Megan laughed. "Always a bridesmaid, never—"

"Shut up," Bella said sharply, elbowing her.

Yikes. Yikes on so many levels. Yikes on bikes. Yikes on this haunted hike. Neither Lauren nor Bella seemed to like Megan, and less so the more champagne they drank. They'd shot little verbal jabs her way for the last couple of hours.

Would there be an issue later on? I'd planned on staying at the inn this weekend to make sure the guests had all they needed, but this seemed more like a teenage sleepover, complete with melodramatic angst.

"I'm dropping you off here then will park the van, okay?" I said. "Stand with the group and I'll meet up with you in a couple of minutes."

"One question," Bella said.

"Of course!"

"The other bridesmaid, Nia, I've been texting with her. I'm going to send her the location here in case she gets into town soon. She's on her way and driving like a maniac. What's the address? Is it okay if she meets us here?"

"She's gonna kill someone," mumbled Megan.

Bella and Lauren ignored her.

"Sure, I guess that's fine," I said, reciting the address. "But I'm afraid no one will be here at the entrance, and I'd hate to have her walk on the path alone in the dark. It might be best to tell her to meet us at the hotel in a couple of hours. She can always go downtown in the meantime. There are shops, restaurants, and bars." I went on to list a few that I'd tried and liked over the weeks.

"Okay."

The three women didn't acknowledge my recommendations or offer a thank you as they scrambled out of the vehicle, but they had a lot to say about Oliver.

"Ew, he's too old. Look at him," Bella muttered. "What is he, like fifty?"

Hey, I wanted to say sharply, *someday you'll be fifty*. But I couldn't. They were paying guests and I needed to get used to this kind of thing.

"Beggars can't be choosers," Lauren retorted. "I'm thirsty. In more ways than one."

Once they'd pulled the back door shut, I sighed and navigated toward the large parking lot. The fact that Lauren lusted after Oliver made sense — he had a certain allure, like a nerdy, handsome professor. Or a slightly scatterbrained bookworm. Which is exactly what he was: a writer of historical accounts of the town, and a professor at a nearby college.

I thought he had shades of Harrison Ford in the first Indiana Jones movie, but perhaps that was my age showing. Regardless, my little crush on Oliver was just that: an infatuation. We'd been out to dinner once, and it turned weird — as everything did in this town, it seemed.

Our date had ended in a chaste cheek kiss. Okay, and plenty of longing looks.

Still, I couldn't wait to hear his ghost stories. I bounded out of the van and joined the group. By the time I reached everyone, the bridesmaids were chatting with Oliver. Helena was also there, and three women I didn't recognize. Must be Helena's guests, I thought.

"Hey, you," Oliver said with a dazzling smile.

Every woman in the group turned to look at me. Then they

quickly returned to Oliver. A pang of sadness went through me. I'd experienced this since turning forty, the invisibility cloak. It's as if society simply stopped noticing women over a certain age.

This kind of treatment from men was regrettable but also understandable, because most men were pigs. But from women — especially younger women — it stung.

I shoved all that into the corners of my brain and went to stand next to Oliver. He turned to me.

"How's it going?" He studied my face. That was what I liked about Oliver: he asked questions and really listened. Some men I'd dated since my divorce droned on and on about themselves.

"Pretty okay," I said with a smile. "We had happy hour at the inn and the bridal party finished off a few bottles of champagne."

"And brought a few with them, I can see." Oliver's gaze went to Lauren, who was handing an open bottle to the other group of bachelorettes. Bella, who was still wearing the tiara, clapped excitedly. A woman with dark hair and a sash that said BRIDE TO BE accepted the bottle and tried to tip it to her mouth but her sash got in the way.

Bella arranged it around her shoulder as Oliver and I watched. Then they poured the contents into an oversized water bottle.

"Teamwork makes the dream work," he observed dryly, and I giggled.

My laughter quickly stopped when a small woman approached. It was Helena. For some reason, she made me feel like I needed to act more buttoned up and mature. Which was odd, since she was at least twenty years younger. She gave off an efficient, know-it-all vibe, especially with the Bluetooth earpiece in her right ear.

She seemed to always act as though she was coordinating a presidential visit.

"I'm so glad you and your guests could join us." She held her arms open for a hug. Even though I'm not much of a hugger, I obliged because she'd done me a massive favor.

When I went in for a casual, quick embrace, I was surprised at the force of her strength.

"Thanks for saving my bacon," I said. "I think my bachelorettes are really going to enjoy this."

"If they remain upright after all that champagne," she murmured, then added, "Just kidding!"

Helena, Oliver, and I huddled for a second to discuss how the walk would unfold.

"As we discussed in the email thread, I'll begin with a wedding-themed ghost story," Oliver said. "Something quick, something a little spooky. There's a clearing a couple hundred feet into the trail, where it forks. We can stop there as a group and I'll tell the story."

"Sounds great to me. How about you, Helena?"

She was staring at Oliver with a loopy grin on her face. Oh, no. Not her, too. He seemed to have a way of captivating women with just a smile. I couldn't be upset because he didn't encourage their affections. He seemed a little oblivious, possibly because he hadn't taken his eyes off me since I walked up.

There was an awkward pause. "Helena?" Oliver finally said gently.

"Oh! Yes. That's a great plan. Perfect." She smoothed her sleek ponytail. Somehow, she managed to look like a country club member, if there was such a thing as a goth country club. She wore a preppy-looking black polo shirt, a black golf skirt made of a synthetic fabric, and black sneakers. She even had little black ruffled ankle socks.

Sporty, yet goth.

Around her neck was a simple gold necklace, and in her ears, cute gold earrings in the shape of bats.

"Well, let's get this show on the road," Helena said, hoisting a large, black leather satchel over her shoulder.

She stepped toward the group, leaving Oliver and I standing alone.

"How's it really going?" he asked out of the corner of his mouth. "You look stressed."

I inhaled deeply. "I am. There's some conflict in my bachelorette party, but nothing that's out of the ordinary. Typical bridezilla stuff. They are intent on drinking a lot of champagne, though."

We snapped to attention because Helena was motioning for us to gather in a large circle.

"Come in closer so you can hear me," she boomed.

We all complied. While Helena introduced us, I scanned the group. Liz had arrived, with Sage and Jimbo. Sage was still in her costume, and Jimbo still looked like... Jimbo. I was surprised Liz had showed up. She'd mentioned something about theater practice — she was in a local thespian group and they were putting on a special fall production of a murder mystery, where the entire cast was over fifty years old.

"Ladies, you might be wondering, who all these other people are. And you might have noticed that they are a bachelorette party, just like you." Helena swept her hand in the direction of my three guests. "Well, I stumbled upon Amelia Matthews, the owner of the Crescent Moon Inn, at a local coffee shop. I'll definitely tell you where that is, you need to visit. The coffee shop, not her inn. Anyway, Amelia was there looking like a lost little lamb, asking about ghost tours. Well, since I already had this set up for all y'all, I decided to be generous and invite her and her group along."

Helena looked to me with a smile. I detected a hint of snark in her tone and was reminded of what Liz had said about Helena and my aunt. Since I always feel uncomfortable when people are passive aggressive — my ex-husband was a master at this — I merely nodded and grinned.

"Thank you for inviting us," I replied. "You're a lifesaver."

With people like Helena, I've found, it's best to give them the credit and recognition they crave.

As expected, Helena beamed. "Well, let's get going. I have some flashlights for everyone in this bag."

She opened her tote and kept talking while handing everyone a flashlight. I took one. Oliver didn't because he had his own. Sage came over and grabbed a torch.

"Hey, cowpoke." Sage considered herself a witch and a cowgirl, and her speech was usually peppered with references to both worlds. While unusual at first, I'd gotten used to her quirks and even enjoyed her wicca-meets-Yellowstone vibe. "I tried one of your snickerdoodles and they were scrumdiddlyumptious."

"Thanks."

"Actually..." Sage said in a loud whisper, "I ate four. And I have some in my purse. Hope you don't mind."

I tried, and failed, to hold back a snort-laugh. "Not in the least."

Helena shot us a stern look as we all wandered toward the trail in a group. "Let's all focus and listen to nature while we walk to the boardwalk. We're going to walk for a few minutes and begin the haunted tour, then our town's historian Oliver Everhart will tell us a ghost story."

I felt oddly chastised, and once again, was reminded of Liz's warnings about her.

The group cheered and I overheard one woman say to

another, "I'd like that Oliver guy to tell me a different kind of story, know what I mean?"

Hoo boy. Helena had a sour look on her face, and I noticed she was staring in the direction of Liz. I edged toward my friend and we dropped back, behind the rest of the group.

"Y'all ready?" I whispered to Liz.

"I love how you're saying *y'all* a lot, it's like you've been in Florida your whole life and not three weeks," Liz cackled. She then leaned into my ear. "I'm gonna take off. I can't handle all the nasty vibes from Helena."

We exchanged mortified glances. "Sorry," I whispered.

"No, don't be sorry. You didn't know. I'm headed over to the theater anyway. We'll chat tomorrow."

We quickly hugged and Liz slipped away, back toward the parking lot. Passing Bella and the bridesmaids with a smile — and having all of them ignore me — I fell into step beside Oliver. We were at the front of the group.

"What is this place, anyway? Is it a private park? Or the county?" I asked.

"It's owned by the town, one of the rare things they did decades ago with an eye for conservation as opposed to development. I'm sure you've noticed that Florida doesn't exactly preserve its historical structures well."

"I have noticed a lot of development in places where maybe there shouldn't be. But California was no different."

Oliver explained that the park was home to not only a swamp, but thousands of Cypress trees with their distinctive flared base and "knees," or the knobby outgrowths of the shallow, horizontal roots.

"Cypress swamps make up about ten percent of Florida," Oliver said.

We talked about the trees for a few minutes as we walked down an asphalt path. I was used to dramatic parks like

Yosemite and Joshua Tree. While pretty and a little spooky in the fading daylight, this seemed like any town park to me.

When we reached a fork in the path, we stopped. For a brief second, no one spoke and the loud hum of cicadas filled the air.

Oliver cleared his throat and everyone looked towards him. I couldn't help but smile as he introduced himself, cracking self-deprecating jokes along the way.

"We're headed onto a wooden boardwalk that will allow us to walk through the swamp without getting wet. The boardwalk is actually a big circle, so we enter here," he gestured to the trail on the right, where a sign said ENTER. "And come out over there."

He pointed to the left, where the sign said EXIT. "Halfway through is a surprise I think you'll enjoy. Now, on our way to the surprise, you might encounter various, ah, *creatures*."

Everyone squealed and clapped with delight.

"After the surprise, there won't be any creatures, but there will be plenty of opportunities for photos. But before we set out, I want to tell you about a ghost in this very swamp. Now, this involves a wedding. Do you all want to hear it?"

A loud and resounding YES cut through the silence. These women were primed for spookiness.

Oliver grinned and nodded. "Okay, here goes. Back in the 1920s, a young woman named Mary Claire Hunt lived on the edge of this swamp, in a little shack with her parents and siblings. She met the man of her dreams and was supposed to get married here. Right in this area, actually. This was before the town bought the land. Back then there was a wooden platform a little ways in, and people in town often came here for wedding photos because of the pretty backdrop."

He gestured with his hand toward the trail that went to the right. "On the day of her wedding, she ventured out early in the morning. She was wearing her wedding gown and she wanted to pick flowers for her bouquet. At least, that's what she told her parents."

Bella, my bride, raised her hand. "I have a question."

Oliver pointed at her, and I imagined him in class, intense and focused. "Yes?"

"Why didn't she just use a florist? That's way easier."

I glanced over at Helena, who was now standing next to me. Our eyes met and we both bit our lips, trying not to laugh.

Oliver didn't flinch, wince, or laugh. Probably he was used to all sorts of questions as a professor. "Cypress Grove was a small town back then. Not even a thousand people. They didn't have a florist, and even if they did, Mary Claire and her family likely couldn't afford such luxuries."

"Sucks," Megan muttered.

"What happened to Lily Claire?" Lauren asked. She was wielding a selfie stick and extended her arm. At first, I thought she was trying to get a good shot of Oliver, but then she and Bella made duck faces and peace signs for the camera.

Attention spans were getting shorter by the day, it seemed.

"Yes, Mary Claire," Oliver corrected, ignoring the selfie session. "She never returned. Her fiancé and the wedding guests waited. And waited. They sent out a search party but didn't find her.

Days later, her body was found floating in the swamp, tangled in the twisted mangrove roots."

"That's so sad," one of Helena's bridesmaids said.

"There's a bit more to the story," Oliver added. "Apparently, Mary Claire wasn't thrilled about the wedding. Her father had arranged the marriage, and there was a rumor that she wasn't here to pick flowers. She was here to end her life. She wasn't in love with her fiancé — but she was in love with someone else. A man named Gerald Gervais. He committed suicide here a week after Mary Claire was found. Took a lethal dose of poison."

"It's like Romeo and Juliet," whispered Bella.

Megan rolled her eyes and sipped from a flask.

"Now their spirits haunt this swamp, floating between the trees in formal clothes," Oliver said. "So, watch for any signs of them on our walk tonight. Who knows? They just might show up this evening and give you some marriage advice."

Three

Even though I wasn't that impressed when I first walked into the park, things quickly changed when we stepped onto the wooden boardwalk. The path was surrounded on two sides by cypress trees, and every so often, I heard the hoot of an owl. The place seemed wild and magical in the semidarkness.

I walked next to Oliver, which meant we were leading the group.

Well, perhaps "leading" was a stretch. We strolled at a slow pace while the rest of the group giggled, drank, skipped, and at one point, three of them sat on the boardwalk to check their phones.

Helena brought up the rear, mostly because she too was on her phone. She'd waved us on and said she'd catch up with us in a few minutes. In the middle were the two brides-to-be and their bridesmaids.

"Folks, we can take this at our own pace. Don't worry about staying together as a group, this is a safe park in a safe community," Oliver said. "We'll meet in about ten minutes down the trail and I'll tell you another story. But please don't go over the side of the railing. That's swamp down there, and that's where the gators live."

"We don't want to lose any of you," I quipped. Everyone laughed. "Take only photos! Leave only memories!"

Oliver and I strolled away, leaving the two bachelorette groups to their tipsy selves. Part of the reason I enjoyed being around him was his easy demeanor. After two decades with my ex, who grew to nitpick every detail in our lives, spending time with people who were positive was a novel experience.

"I think it's good if we give them some space, while making sure no one does anything stupid," I said. "But this place is quite fascinating. What's the surprise?"

"It wouldn't be a surprise if I told you," Oliver said in a teasing tone. "You're going to lose your mind at how beautiful it is."

"Cool," I said with a grin.

For some reason, I had expected the walkway to be something makeshift and shoddy. This was a well-constructed wood path, wide enough for three people to walk side-by-side, with wooden railings on both sides.

Every few hundred feet was a small viewing platform, and I imagined that during the day, people would be treated to a view of birds, gators, and the prehistoric-looking cypress trees. Tonight, though, the trees were ominous shadows and the wildlife hidden.

It was legitimately spooky, and that was before I saw the zombie.

"Braiiiiiins," it shouted, and I yelped. Somehow, the person dressed in raggedy clothes and green-gray makeup had managed to perch atop a bench at one of the viewing platforms, looking like a terrifying gargoyle.

I screamed, hid my face in my hands, and turned smack into Oliver's broad chest. He chuckled and wrapped an arm around me, folding me into an awkward half hug. We were close enough so that I could smell his spicy aftershave.

As much as I didn't want to, I pulled away. "Sorry. That was a shock. I wasn't anticipating that. Now I know what's going on here. Okay. I've got this."

Oliver thanked the performer, who gave us a little salute, and we resumed walking. The women behind us laughed and yelped, then all clustered around the zombie for photos.

"I brought a ring light," Lauren called out.

Oliver and I stood and watched as Bella and Lauren posed for photos with the costumed performer. Megan and Helena's guests stood aside and drank. The women all seemed so... young.

"It's a lot different than when I had my wedding," I observed. "This group doesn't even seem old enough to legally get married, but..."

My words ended in a sigh. Suddenly I felt old as dirt.

"But?"

Oliver and I resumed our saunter. "But I guess I was their age when I married my ex."

"Did you have a bachelorette party?"

I snorted. "My coworkers threw a party. There was a male stripper dressed as a pizza guy. He knocked on the door in uniform, carrying a pizza box. I was so excited about the pizza, but he wasn't convincing as a sex god. And the pizza box was empty, much to my disappointment. Oh, and then he stayed while we ordered takeout Chinese and ate all the moo shu pork while in his G-string."

Oliver was cracking up and I loved the sound so much that I continued with my tragic comedy routine. "And if that wasn't a sign that I shouldn't get married, how about this: my florist hit on me. While I was talking to him about my wedding bouquet."

"What? Noooo!" He wiped a tear from his eye and continued laughing.

"Yep. I went to visit the florist two days before the wedding to make sure everything was set. He was from Russia and informed me that I shouldn't be marrying 'that jerk guy' and that when we got divorced, I should immediately return to his shop and go out with him."

"Wow. Wow. Well, did you?"

"Date the guy after my divorce? Heck no. In retrospect, it was a sign I shouldn't have married my ex, but hindsight is 20/20. Honestly, though, I'm in a good place about my divorce. Really excited to be starting fresh here in Cypress Grove."

"I know Sage and Liz are happy to have you here. And I'm glad, too."

His words sent little prickles of awareness through me. No sooner was I grooving with that happy feeling when I was surprised by a mummy on one of the platforms. This time, I didn't yelp or reach for Oliver (although I wanted to).

All I did was laugh and laugh. This continued for several minutes. We'd walk and talk, then stumble upon a costumed creature. The more memorable — and less gory — creatures included a mummy, a werewolf, and a vampire that was both short and slight. A cute vampire.

The performers really were something, with detailed and lifelike costumes. It made sense, though, if they had access to the theme park resources. My mind spun with various ideas on how to hire people for events at the inn.

"That looks like real blood," I shouted to Oliver, over the wails of a woman holding a scarlet-tipped knife. The sounds of the bridesmaids behind us yelping and screaming with laughter echoed through the night air.

"This is so fun," I squealed when Oliver and I came to a

stop. It was time for his second ghost story. We waited until most of the group was there, but I noticed that Helena was missing.

Probably on her phone.

Oliver cleared his throat as the group formed a loose circle around us. "For my next tale, we'll go back a few decades to the 1950s here in Cypress Grove. There was a young woman named Betty who worked as a waitress at a diner. She was known for her sweet personality and stellar service. She'd always give generous portions of pie. That diner's still here, by the way, and the pie's still excellent."

The bridesmaids quieted down, enthralled by Oliver's oratory skills. Or his muscular forearms. I wasn't sure which. He sure did know how to emphasize certain words for effect. I wondered where he picked that up.

"One night after closing up, Betty was walking home alone near downtown. The moon was full and bright, illuminating the palm trees all around. As Betty walked, she heard a strange noise behind her. Turning around, she saw nothing but shadows."

I leaned in, completely immersed.

Oliver continued, in a hushed, dramatic tone. "Betty shrugged it off and kept walking. But then came another odd sound, like a whisper in her ear. She spun around and thought she glimpsed a dark figure duck behind a tree. Betty broke into a run. The sidewalk seemed to stretch on endlessly before her."

"Just as Betty was contemplating knocking on the door of a nearby home, a cold, clammy hand clamped down on her shoulder. She opened her mouth to scream but no sound came out. Slowly, she looked behind her and saw...nothing. The hand released its grip. Betty was alone."

The tension swirling in the air was palpable. For the first time this evening, no one was looking at their cell phones.

"Shaking with fear, Betty sprinted the rest of the way. When she got home, she noticed red marks on her shoulder. From that night on, she never walked home alone again. Some say the ghostly hand still reaches out to unsuspecting visitors around town, looking for its next victim. So be careful when you're walking in Cypress Grove."

The women gasped and murmured to each other, vowing to only go anywhere in a group. I wasn't sure if Oliver was recounting a real event or if he'd made it up. Either way, I was impressed with his storytelling skills.

"That was so creepy and awesome!" Bella exclaimed. "I'll never look at this place the same way again."

Megan took a long pull from her flask. "Ghosts aren't real," she slurred. "We're all just random collections of particles drifting through an endless void."

A troubling silence followed her gloomy proclamation.

"Well, then," I said brightly, "Shall we keep going and see what surprises are next?"

Oliver and I strolled on, chatting about everything from the diner's best pie (key lime) to the love calls of alligators (it wasn't mating season, so I wouldn't hear any this evening, much to my relief). We seemed to leave the others behind, but we could sure hear them. It warmed my heart to know that my guests were having an incredible time before such a momentous occasion.

This innkeeping career was turning out to be extremely fun. Who knew? Obviously, my aunt had, and I was proud to continue her legacy in town. Endless fun and hilarious possibilities and ideas stretched before me. But my practical side soon emerged.

"Should we be worried about separating from the group? I don't know if I should be more of a chaperone or stay hands off. Or maybe Sage and Jimbo are keeping an eye on them."

Oliver glanced at me. "No, I don't think they need constant monitoring. They're adults, and unless they do something really stupid, they'll be fine. It's not like they can get lost. The boardwalk is a circle and it all leads back to the parking lot."

He was a college professor, and the guests' ages were closer to that of his students, so I couldn't argue with his logic.

"I'm used to being with my daughter, and I think she always needs monitoring," I said with a laugh. "That's the mom in me."

Our conversation was interspersed with interruptions from various costumed creatures, although as we went on, they seemed to be more cute than scary. Swamp creatures, bayou witches, Bigfoot... all were clad in beautifully detailed costumes, but the adrenaline rush of seeing them in the middle of the swamp had eased up. Although Oliver said the trail wasn't that long in distance, it seemed to stretch on and on because we were dawdling and talking. Not that I minded. More than an hour passed, and when Oliver wasn't explaining all sorts of interesting history about the town, we were laughing, telling jokes and having a blast.

"Okay, we're coming up on the surprise, it's right around this bend."

"Oooh, I can't wait!"

"Let's do this: you close your eyes, and I'll lead you to it. I won't let you bump into anything, and there's no more platforms so there won't be any characters in costumes to surprise us. Helena didn't want any characters up ahead there so I could tell the scariest story in the near darkness."

"Sounds pretty spooky." I glanced at him, and he looked so earnest and eager that I couldn't say no.

"Here, take my hand." He held his out, and I reached for it.

I felt a little jolt when we touched, not unlike when I used my psychometry powers. We threaded our fingers together. Dang, this felt good. My ex hated holding hands, claiming I was "too sweaty."

"Sorry if my palm is perspiring."

"I don't care about that at all. Close your eyes," he said softly, and something in my stomach clenched in a delicious way. I hadn't felt that in a long, long time.

"Okay, let's take it slow. One step at a time. Just trust me."

It wasn't easy for me to trust, especially a man. But something about Oliver was different. Smiling, I took a step, then another. The place seemed exceptionally spooky now that I couldn't see, and the humid night air combined with the sounds of the cicadas seemed ominous for some reason.

"Good, good, you're doing well. You're not peeking, are you?"

"No," I said. My eyes were squeezed tight.

"Okay, let's go a little to the left, yes, just like that. Excellent. Only a few more steps. Easy, now."

We took five steps. What would the others say if they saw us? Sage would certainly tease me. Where were the others? I guess Oliver and I walked faster and further than the group. Or they were futzing around on the trail with the characters. Probably taking selfies.

"Can I open my eyes?"

"I'll give you the cue. Two more steps. In three, two, oh whoa, what the hell is that?"

My eyes flew open. The first thing I saw was a pond, silvery in the partial moonlight and ringed with Cypress trees. The second thing I saw was a cute little beach. It looked possibly man made, because why else would there be a strip of sand near a pond in the middle of a swamp? Florida was so weird.

Then I saw something on the shore near a palm tree, lying

in a twisted, unnatural way. It looked alarmingly like a human being.

"Oh no," I yelled, pulling my hand out of Oliver's grip.

I surged forward, bounding down three steps to the small beach. I had to help that poor person.

"Amelia, be careful," he shouted.

"Come on, they need help," I yelled to Oliver and anyone else within earshot. "Call 911! Now!"

But when I reached the person, three horrible things came into sharp focus.

One, it was a woman.

Two, no one could survive ... whatever happened.

And three, it was Megan, one of my guests.

Four

The next several moments were absolute mayhem. They unfolded in excruciating slow motion.

First, I hyperventilated while leaning against a sign explaining the flora and fauna in the pond. Oliver tried to simultaneously dial 911 and calm me down. I nearly threw up, but thankfully didn't. That was all I needed tonight, him seeing me in *that* state.

Then when he got off the phone, he started to clear his throat and tried to take several deep breaths. He squeezed his eyes shut. Beads of perspiration formed on his forehead.

"Are you okay?" I asked. "Wait, that's a stupid question. Obviously, you're not okay. How *could* you be okay?"

He whispered that he was having a mild anxiety attack. I admired him even more for admitting that, since sometimes men had difficulties with their emotions.

"It's going to be fine," I said, running my hands up and down his arms. All the while, Megan's body was in my peripheral vision. I stepped to the left, so I didn't have to look at it. As it was, my insides were shaking like an 8.0 earthquake.

Oliver looked so upset — and I was equally as devastated — that I wrapped my arms around him, seeking solace. He hugged me back. We stayed like that for a couple of minutes, then I reluctantly pulled away.

He scrubbed his face with his hands. "Okay. Everything will be fine. We need to tell ourselves that. My God, it's horrible, seeing her. But we're going to get through this. We're going to be okay." He was trying to reassure me, and himself.

Would we, though? Usually when people had to repeatedly tell themselves that things were fine, things were usually pretty rotten. At least that's what I'd experienced during my forty-seven years.

"Have you ever seen a dead body?" I hissed, even though we were the only ones on the beach.

Well, the only living ones.

He shook his head. "Just in funeral homes."

"Same."

We huddled by the sign, silently freaking out and reassuring each other. That's when the burble of voices hit our ears. Flashlight beams bobbed in the air near the path. I'd forgotten all about the others.

"Oh, crap," he said. "Stay here."

I watched as he sprinted over the hard-packed sand to the steps leading to the boardwalk. It was the guests, and they were about to get the shock of their lives. I, too, scrambled into a run.

Or tried to. My legs felt like heavy rubber, and they tangled in the skirt of my cute black ghost dress. I slid and slipped on a patch of wet algae. My entire body went flying and landed flat on my backside. No one noticed, I didn't care, and awkwardly rolled around then got back up. My body suffered only a little.

Maybe more than a little, but I didn't have time to dwell on the pain throbbing in my hip. Or the fact that I smelled like clammy algae. Oliver and I had to intercept the bridal party before they saw Megan.

"Stop," I hollered. My voice sounded small in the darkness. "Don't walk on the beach!"

"What is that? Why can't we go out on the beach? Oh my god, Bella, that's Megan!" Lauren screamed at the top of her lungs and barreled toward the body. "Megan, are you okay? I think she's really drunk and she passed out!"

"Noooo, stop!" I cried, my arms flailing in the air. Small clumps of green algae tumbled from my clothes.

"Lauren, don't go over there." Oliver's calm voice sliced through the air. He'd obviously summoned a well of courage and mental stability, whereas I was a total disaster.

It was too late, however.

Lauren, Bella, and the other bridal party clustered around Megan's body. Sage and Jimbo came running up, seemingly out of nowhere. Where had they been? Who knew with those two, though. Nothing would surprise me about them.

"What's going on?" Jimbo asked.

"Uh-oh," Sage said, taking off her giant blue hat. "That looks… not okay."

"She doesn't seem drunk," Bella said. "She definitely looks dead."

I couldn't stand watching, or hearing, the women and their unfolding, justified horror.

This was a situation that demanded a level head. What was my most challenging moment as a parent? I needed to summon that vibe.

There was a time when a bat got inside my home in Sonoma, while my then-twelve-year-old daughter was having a sleepover with eight of her friends. Since the kids discovered the bat, they freaked out. I did, too, with visions of my daughter's painful death from rabies. And since my husband was out of town at a bakery trade show convention (I later found out he was sleeping with a rep from an artisan frosting company), I had to woman up and deal with the situation.

Just as I needed to right now.

With a deep, fortifying breath, I marched over to the group. While trying not to look at Megan's twisted body, I clapped my hands.

That seemed to startle the women enough to look at me.

"We need to step away from here so the authorities can do their jobs. Come with me. Right now. This is a terrible situation but we need to back away to let the police work. They'll be here any second." I used my most stern mom voice, and it seemed to work because all five women dutifully followed me back to the boardwalk entrance.

We all stood in three groups: Oliver, Jimbo, Sage, and me. Lauren and Bella. The other group were Helena's guests. That jogged my memory.

"Has anyone seen Helena?" I asked.

"We were dawdling, looking at a gator, and she passed us. Said she was on her way back to the car to make a call. Her cell wasn't getting good reception out here," Jimbo said.

"Weird," Oliver muttered.

I was going to ask him why when the sound of what sounded like tires on wood planks filled the air. We all turned in the direction of the boardwalk in time to see a half-dozen bright lights coming from the wooden walkway.

It was the Cypress Grove Police, on bicycles. The first one sailed off the boardwalk, skipping the three steps down to the beach in an airborne wheelie. He came to a fast stop, tossed the bicycle on the ground, and marched up to us while taking off his helmet.

The man was unusually large, his voice a low growl.

Without shifting his eyes off me, he handed the helmet to another officer standing a few paces behind.

"I'm Chief Christopher Wolf. I understand you've got a dead body on your hands." His eyes seemed to take us all in with suspicion as he sized us up. The chief looked to be around my age, possibly a few years younger. He had the look of a man who had spent decades honing and sculpting his physique.

"Actually, the body's over there, and none of us have touched it," Sage offered.

Wolf studied her as if she'd sprouted a third arm before his very eyes. "10-4. What's going on out here, anyway? What is all this?"

He gestured dismissively at Sage's costume, which annoyed me for some reason. Since I was the de facto leader of this band of misfits, I stepped forward.

"I'm Amelia Matthews, the owner of the Crescent Moon Inn." The chief's skeptical gaze made me feel like I'd done something wrong. I held out my hand. He didn't take it.

"Okay. Nice to meet you, ma'am. Again, my question is: what's going on out here? Why are you all in a town park in the middle of the night in costumes and tiaras? Who were all those performers in the parking lot? My guys almost ran them over."

"Oh, dear. I'm sorry." I wrung my hands. "This is a bachelorette party. Well, two bachelorette parties. Three are staying at another place and three... well, the others, are staying at my inn. The owner of another hotel and I collaborated and she asked her friends the theme park performers to dress up in costu—"

"I get it. Save the details for the official interview." he said brusquely. "Where's the other hotel owner? Is there anyone else in your party who's not here?"

"No. Everyone's here. Except Helena."

The chief sighed heavily.

"Oh no, what if something happened to Helena? What if the killer got her too?" The questions came from one of the bridesmaids staying at the Lakeview. She was in tears.

"Ma'am, we'll get to the bottom of this. Please try to remain calm."

He put his hands on his hips and in a flash, an intense spotlight shone on his face. I looked over and saw an officer adjusting a floodlight. How had he gotten it here on a bicycle? I guess the police had their special gadgets.

"My men will question all of you separately while I inspect the body and consult with the ME. You all stay where you are, and don't talk to each other about this case. I'd prefer you not speak to each other at all." He fixed a stern eye on me. "Copy that?"

Why was he using police dispatcher lingo in regular conversation? I nodded slowly.

"Excuse me." It was Lauren. Her right hand was in the air, like she was in class. Her left hand was twirling a lock of her hair. A half smile spread on her face, as if she was trying to flirt. Eek. Bizarre.

Wolf's eyes narrowed. "This isn't a Q and A session."

"What do you mean by the emm-eee? Is that like a new app?"

We all gaped at her. Wolf blinked slowly. His chiseled jaw worked back and forth, as if he was grinding his molars. "No. It's two letters. M and E. Short for medical examiner. Now if you'll excuse me, I have a death investigation to begin."

Chastised, she turned back to Bella, who shot her a nasty look.

While Wolf walked away, I angled myself to face Oliver, Sage, and Jimbo. "Is that the guy who's allegedly a werewolf?"

"Yes," Sage whispered. "Doesn't he look like one? Can't you imagine hair sprouting from those huge hands of his?

Thank the goddess it's not a full moon tonight. He's already a handful."

"I don't see werewolf, but what do I know," I replied, glancing over at him. Chief Wolf stood over the body while scratching his head. "He looks like a guy who goes to the gym a lot."

And one who hopefully had a good dentist on speed dial, if that teeth grinding was an everyday thing.

"Lotta those cops do, and prison guards," chimed in Jimbo. "Did you know there's a whole exercisin' routine called the Prison Workout? Some guy from England was locked up and he invented it."

The three of us stared at Jimbo, whose face was open and relaxed in the spotlight. Sometimes with him, I didn't know how to respond. I felt the same way about Sage, too. Come to think of it, they made a great pair, even if they were a little scattered and odd. I didn't know if either was even single, and now was probably not the best time to ask.

I shook my head, trying to clear my jumbled thoughts.

"Amelia, can I have a word with you alone?" Oliver whispered, obviously ignoring Wolf's request that we not talk to each other.

I nodded and we walked a few feet away while Jimbo and Sage chatted about prisons. They, too, didn't seem that worked up about Wolf's order.

"This is super weird," Oliver said out of the corner of his mouth. "I don't feel good about this."

"So weird. What do you think happened?"

He raked his hand through his black hair. "It doesn't look like natural causes, that's for sure. Did you see her neck?"

I winced. I had, indeed, seen the fresh marks. "You think it's murder?"

"Sure seems like it. But who would murder... what was her

name? That's awful of me. I don't even remember." Oliver shook his head, looking miserable.

"Megan. I don't recall her last name right now, I'm so discombobulated. All I know is that she's from Orlando like the bride and groom. I think she's a member of the groom's family. Or the bride. I don't know. A cousin? I don't know. The other two didn't seem to like her. But would they kill her?"

"I don't see how they could have. Unless they ran all the way back and around the other way, then returned. No one passed *us* on the boardwalk so Megan had to go around the other part of the loop. Then again, it's really not that far. We all just took it slow. I come here to run and the full circle is two miles. I can do the whole thing in about eighteen minutes."

I stared at him for a second. Nine minutes a mile seemed fast to me, but then again, Oliver was pretty fit. "Hmm. Wouldn't the performers have seen Megan?"

Oliver lifted his shoulders. "They were given the okay to leave once our group passed. Then again, they could have seen her, I suppose. But Helena told me there would be no performers from here, at the pond, on the second leg of the loop. There are only folks in costumes on half of the loop, the half we were on. And the performers probably left after we passed. A long way of saying probably not."

"Why didn't Helena want the performers around the entire path?" I scrunched up my nose. Nothing was making sense.

"Before you drove up tonight, she suggested I tell the scariest story here at the pond, then the group would get really scared in the silence on the way back. Plus, there's a dramatic vista on the boardwalk on the way back that's good for selfies. She put a balloon canopy there."

"Makes sense. This is a selfie-loving crowd." Except Megan. She didn't seem like the type to take photos of herself. "And where do you think Helena is? I'm worried about her. She's the only one not here, right?"

I must've spoken in a too-loud tone because Chief Wolf came stomping over.

"Hey! You two. Break it up. What did I say about not discussing the case?"

"But—"

"No buts. Zip it," Wolf said.

Grimacing, I apologized and wandered away from Oliver, back to the tree I'd nearly barfed on. With my back against the trunk, I surveyed the scene unfolding on the beach. It really wasn't that big, but with the nine people on the haunted walk plus the ever-growing police presence, it seemed quite crowded.

Oliver was pacing alone about twenty feet away. Sage and Jimbo were sitting in the sand, staring at the water, seemingly not talking. No, wait, actually they were eating cookies out of her satchel.

A few feet from them sat Bella and Lauren, whispering. The other three women were nearby, their faces illuminated from their phones.

A gaggle of paramedics arrived as did more officers in a fancy, military-looking four-wheeler. I watched them climb out, then to my surprise, realized one was Helena.

"Chief," one of the men called out, then clamped his hand around Helena's upper arm. "We found this woman sitting in her car in the parking lot."

She twisted out of his grip. "Keep your hands off me, you brute. I'm in charge of this situation."

I bit my lip as I watched Chief Wolf stride over. "Excuse me? You're in charge?"

Helena folded her arms over her chest. "Oh. Christopher. Hello."

She didn't appear happy to see him at all. I glanced around

and caught Oliver's gaze. He raised his eyebrows. I widened my eyes. This was juicy.

I shifted my back against the tree, scratching in a pleasurable spot near my shoulder, as I watched the drama.

"Helena, I should've known you were behind this. What gave you the idea to come out here in the middle of the night?"

"It's only nine p.m., sir," Sage called out.

I stifled a laugh. Sage, whether she intended or not, was hilarious with her obvious observations.

The chief ignored her. "Did you even get a permit for this?"

She rolled her eyes. "Negative. I only did it because the other inn owner wanted to team up."

I gaped and gasped. That was not the truth at all.

"Where is she hiding, anyway?" Helena swiveled her head.

I stepped forward, out of the shadows. It made me feel dramatic and slightly ridiculous. "Here I am," I said in a higher-than-usual pitch.

Helena beckoned. "Hey, lady! Tell the chief about how we collaborated on this. How you were looking for a haunted walk for your guests."

When I reached them, I looked only at Wolf. "It's true that I was looking for a haunted event for my guests. Helena was the one who invited me to join her."

The chief stared at me and shook his head. Without saying a word, he turned and walked away. Now I was thoroughly baffled. I shifted my attention to Helena.

"What's going on?" I said in a low tone.

She shook her head. "Christopher and I went out on a date when he first arrived in town."

My lower jaw dropped, making me look like a grouper. "Oh. Oh dear. Well. I'm sure that won't affect the investigation. Or will it? I don't know how these things work. I've never been involved with the law before..."

My voice trailed off, squashed by her withering glare.

What the duck is going on here? Why is she telling me this? Why is she looking at me like that?

"Let's just hope he's a better investigator than a lover," she said darkly. "Excuse me, I need to chat with my guests."

With that, she pivoted on the ball of her foot and walked across the sand, leaving me speechless.

Five

One police interview, one sad trudge back to the van, a tense drive back to the inn, and three snickerdoodle cookies later, I exhaled in the lobby, finally alone. I'd changed out of my sand-and-algae covered clothes, into a cozy sweatshirt and yoga pants.

Bella and Lauren were upstairs in their room, and I was worried as heck about them. Both were quiet on the short drive back in the van, and it was obvious they were stunned at the tragic turn of events, as we all were.

Bella, especially, seemed to be taking it quite hard. She'd even left a long and rambling message for her fiancé while we were walking into the inn.

Chief Wolf told them not to leave town. Told all of us that, actually. The two women were at first reluctant to stay at the Crescent Moon, but when they realized all other hotels were booked, and that I still had booze and cookies, they agreed to return with me.

Oliver was driving Sage and Jimbo home, and he'd promised to return to check on me.

I let out a long sigh, double locked the front door, then went into the library. There, I extracted a book, and the entire shelf slid to the side, revealing an entrance to a cozy living room. My aunt had created this mysterious doorway into her apartment some years back, I was told.

It was a conversation piece, that was for sure. Whether it was practical was a different story, but it would afford me some privacy when I moved here permanently. Plus, it was just plain cool to have a hidden apartment behind a bookshelf. Every time I entered, I felt like a spy, or a character in an adventure novel.

Actually, I'd been feeling like that anyway, ever since coming here. I didn't need a hidden apartment and a moving bookcase for that.

When I stepped into the living room, I was greeted with a loud, plaintive yowl.

"Hey chonker," I said. My cat, Freddie Purrcury, wound his substantial frame around my legs. I reached down to pick him up. "Oof. Dude. So heavy."

He rubbed his face along my chin, marking me with his scent. I toted him under my arm like a package while walking into the kitchen. I grabbed a beer out of the fridge and returned to the living room, releasing Freddie to the floor.

The sofa never felt so good. I cracked open the bottle and took a long sip. It tasted bitter and hoppy. Normally I didn't even like beer but had bought it for the guests.

"What a day, Freddie. What a night. Oof." I shook my head.

Freddie jumped up and crawled in my lap, all four paws digging into my thighs and stomach. He began to knead me softly. I planted a kiss on his broad head then took another long sip.

Setting my beer down on the side table, I sank back into the soft cushions of the sofa. Freddie's kneads became more insistent, with claws.

"Easy there, furry man," I murmured, stroking his fur.

The evening's events replayed in my mind. Screams in the park, the police interviews, the solemn trudge with Oliver and the guests back to the van. A shudder went through me at the memory.

This was not how I intended to begin my new career as an inn owner.

Chief Wolf was right to advise us all to stay put for now. As much as I wanted to forget the whole thing, to carry on as normal, I knew there were still answers to be found. And dangers, perhaps, that I couldn't yet fathom. I hoped not, though.

In my first weeks in Cypress Grove, I'd learned that many, if not most, folks here harbored some sort of extranormal talent. Many were psychics and mediums, while others were witches. I'd seen a long-dead ghost with my own eyes and had experienced intense, long-buried personal memories from the psychometry. If the cops couldn't crack the case, surely one of the many with special abilities could.

Now that a guest had been murdered, things seemed incredibly urgent. And perilous. Hopefully the killer would be caught tonight — although from what I saw of Chief Wolf's increasingly gruff demeanor, I didn't get the impression he was on the verge of cracking the case.

Freddie let out another loud yowl, nipping gently at my hand with his teeth. His behavior was so unusual tonight. Normally he was gentle and lazy. It was like he could sense my unease, my unspoken fears. He wanted comfort and security, too.

"It's alright," I whispered, lifting him against my chest and wrapping my arms around his solid, furry body. His rumbling purr vibrated through me, oddly soothing. "I'm home now. We're safe."

Saying it out loud almost made me believe it. This was supposed to become my sanctuary, the one place where the chaos and uncertainties of the outside world couldn't touch me.

With Freddie still snuggled in my embrace, I moved slowly, taking another sip of bitter beer, feeling my eyelids grow heavy. It was doubtful that I would get any rest, my mind was so worked up.

Maybe I should call Oliver and tell him that I was okay, that he didn't need to come over. As much as I enjoyed his company, this sofa was looking like a comfy place to sleep this evening (I couldn't muster the thought of sleeping in my aunt's bed).

I allowed my eyes to shut. Just for a few minutes. A little rest for my eyes. And my back.

I'd no sooner drifted into a half-sleep with Freddie on my lap when I heard the doorbell. *Bing-bong!* It was louder than expected and it startled me. I surged forward and Freddie leaped off my lap.

"Must be Oliver," I muttered. While rubbing the sleep out of my eyes, I padded through the secret door, into the library and then out into the lobby. Freddie followed close behind.

When I unlocked and opened the door, I was surprised to find it wasn't Oliver.

It was a woman in her twenties that I didn't recognize. She had long, unkempt blonde hair and looked to be wet and muddy. Maybe her car had broken down. Or maybe she'd trekked through a swamp. The hair on my arms stood on end at the thought.

"Can I help you?"

"Hi, I'm Nia. I'm with the bridesmaid party, you know, Bella and Lauren and Megan."

"Oh. Oh!" I'd totally forgotten she was supposed to arrive late. Or at all. Freddie darted out of the room. "Absolutely, come on in."

I stepped aside to let her enter. She toted an expensive-looking piece of designer luggage, and her boots also looked to be the same designer. Louis Vuitton was unmistakable.

She brushed past me, chattering. "I was late getting out of work and then traffic was awful. How does anyone ever commute on I-4? Then wouldn't you know it, I got a flat tire and my cell died. I started to change the tire myself and then a guy stopped to help, then he had all sorts of complications. I couldn't charge my phone because my cord crapped out. I've had the worst luck tonight and I hope the girls are ready to drink because I want to party."

It dawned on me that she knew nothing about the events of the evening. She stood in the lobby, taking it all in.

"Wow, this is cool. Spooky cool. Spooky scary. Spoopy! That's my favorite word. Spoopy! Love the gator, by the way. I didn't catch your name. You are?"

"I'm Amelia Matthews, the owner." I held out my hand and we shook.

"You look about as exhausted as me. Listen, where are my friends? Please don't tell me they went to a bar. I need to relax."

"They're upstairs." I tried to hide my discomfort.

"Oh nice! I'll go up there now. Where is it? Unless you need anything from me, like a credit card? I think I'm supposed to be rooming with Megan. Between us, Lauren hates her. Refused to stay in a room with her."

She made a face that said, *I got the short end of the stick.*

Oh, dear.

"About that," I said as she was about to take the first step on the staircase. "There's something you should know first."

I hesitated, unsure of how to break the news gently. Nia peered at me expectantly, oblivious to the awfulness of the last several hours.

"There was...an incident earlier this evening," I began slowly. "Maybe you should sit."

I gestured to a red velvet loveseat in the corner. She stared hard at me, then eased onto the cushion. I perched on the edge, as far away as I could get.

"We were on the haunted swamp walk. Something happened. I'm afraid it involves your friend Megan."

"She's not my friend. She's Bella's second cousin. They only know each other from their hometown. Some small place near Orlando. Super redneck." She said this in a snotty, arrogant tone.

"Okay, well, whatever. Your roommate. Your fellow bridesmaid."

Nia's brow furrowed. "What kind of incident? Is Megan okay? Is she drunk again?"

I sighed, wrapping my arms around my midsection. The beer was not sitting well in my tummy. "She's not okay. I'm so sorry to have to tell you this, but Megan was found dead by the pond. The police think she was murdered. It happened while we were all walking along the boardwalk."

"What?" Nia gasped, pressing her hands to her cheeks. Her bright blue eyes were wide with shock. "Murdered? Megan's dead?"

I nodded grimly. "I'm afraid so. Somehow, she got separated from the group and ended up near a small pond. The police interviewed all of us earlier, while we were at the pond. I found her first. I'm so sorry, Nia."

She stood frozen for a long moment, shaking her head in

disbelief. Tears welled in her eyes. "I don't understand." Her voice broke on a sob.

Gently, I put a hand on her shoulder. "I know this is a lot to take in. Do you need some water?" She sank back into the velvet loveseat, shoulders slumped in grief.

"I can't believe this," she whispered. Her expression was one of total devastation.

"The police are on the case and they seem quite competent," I explained softly. "They asked us all not to leave town yet. I'm sure they'll want to speak with you too. Do you have parents or a partner, or anyone to call?"

"I need to talk with Bella and Lauren. Where are they?" Tears stained her cheeks.

"I'll take you to them. I'm sorry to have to tell you this information, but I didn't want you to bust in on your friends expecting a party."

"Of course. Thank you for that. You're so sweet." She half-hiccupped, half-sobbed.

"Follow me upstairs." I rubbed her back as we walked to the stairs. As I worked my mom magic to soothe her, I wondered about the other magic.

The psychometry.

I'd noticed in recent days that touching other people didn't yield any memories or visions. It only seemed to happen with objects. I'd have to tell Oliver about this finding — he was fascinated by my ability and had done all sorts of research. He'd even summarized it for me in an email with bullet points, which I thought sweet.

The hallway seemed to stretch on for miles as Nia and I trudged to the final room. I'd put Bella and Lauren in the Lavender and Lace room, figuring the bride should get the largest space.

As we approached, we could hear snippets of conversation. I slowed, out of no other reason than sheer nosiness.

"Do you think she met someone?"

"Who knows? She's so weird. Probably she sank her talons into one of those vampires in the swamp and —"

I was hesitating to knock because I wanted to hear more of the conversation, but Nia shoved open the door like a gator crashing a pool party.

"You guys, I just heard about Megan!" She collapsed into their arms and she and Bella sobbed in tandem. Lauren remained oddly dry-eyed. I remained in the doorway, unsure of what to do or say.

"Girls?" I gave them a little wave, feeling awkward. Something about their raw, visceral emotion was making my maternal instincts kick in. "Would you like me to bring you anything?"

Through an exaggerated sniffle, Lauren glanced over at me. "Another bottle of chilled champagne. Oh, and those cookies." She said it like she was demanding caviar from the Queen's kitchen. "The vegan ones."

"Absolutely. Be right back." I scurried away, eager to do something, anything, for these grieving people. Even if Lauren had treated me like her own personal servant since arriving, she didn't deserve any of this.

I hustled downstairs, my feet barely touching the steps, and prepared a plate of cookies, along with some fruit and crackers. After popping open a bottle of champagne with a hollowly festive boom, it went into a filled ice bucket, and I unearthed a giant tray from my aunt's kitchen.

I moved through the rooms like a pinball, ricocheting from counter to fridge to pantry. There was another, larger kitchen elsewhere in the hotel, and I assumed that was what my aunt had used while cooking for guests. I'd barely had time to explore that space though, so I confined myself to what I did know, which was her living quarters.

Fortunately, her kitchen was a foodie's dream, with shiny gadgets and containers galore. I even discovered cute cocktail napkins embossed with little witches' hats. I added those to the tray along with some chocolate truffles, then started toward the stairs, my arms quivering from the heavy load.

That's when the doorbell rang. Twice. Then three times. Grumbling, I carefully navigated to the lobby, shoulders screaming, then perched the tray on the desk. I flung open the door with the fury of someone expecting bad news. It was Oliver.

"Hey. You okay?" Since he was about a foot taller than me, he looked down with an expression of concern.

"Hanging in there." I blew out a long breath. Exhaustion was setting in. "I have to bring this tray up to the guests. The other bridesmaid just arrived. Want to meet me in the apartment? There's beer in the fridge. And snacks."

"That's the best news I've heard all night. See you in a few." His smile was a much-needed lift to my spirits.

We crossed paths and I went upstairs, moving slow. Mostly because I didn't want to dump the champagne on the hallway floor and create a sticky slip-n-slide, but also so I could eavesdrop.

The tray grew heavier with each step, straining my noodle-like arms. I vowed that when I finally got settled here in town, I'd join a gym. Being a weakling was no way to begin midlife.

I heard the women's voices drift from the room.

"Do you honestly think she just took off with some guy she met? She was stupid but not that stupid," Lauren's vocal fry was unmistakable.

"That doesn't seem like Megan," Bella replied.

A third voice that I recognized as Nia's piped up. "You

never know with her. She was always chasing men. She was into some pretty kinky stuff."

I leaned closer, ears perked. Their conversation seemed to hint that the reasons for Megan's death were complicated. Or was I reading too much into things? Maybe my peri-menopausal brain was misfiring, as it sometimes did.

Just then, a loud thump sounded behind me in the hall, making me jump. The tray wobbled dangerously in my hands and the ice in the bucket rattled. What was that? I crept toward the noise.

Pressing my ear to the supply closet door, I heard a rustling sound, like something moving inside. My pulse quickened. Was the killer hiding in there? Holding my breath, I reached for the handle, the tray wobbling in one hand.

Get a grip, I told myself. It was probably a mouse. Or something fell. Crud. There was no way I could hold this thing with one hand. I carefully slid my other palm to help cradle the tray.

I made a mental note to check the closet later as I retraced my steps, hurrying to deliver the refreshments before my hands gave out or my lower back seized up. While eavesdropping had provided an interesting possible clue, I couldn't let my imagination run away with me.

The door flung open even before I knocked. Lauren peeked out, startling me so much that I nearly dropped the tray.

It was a miracle that I didn't.

"Oh, you're finally here. Great." She spoke in an odd, gravelly, monotone. "Put it on the bed."

"Gosh, Lauren, you could say please." Even Bella seemed annoyed that Lauren was acting so haughty.

In response, Lauren rolled her eyes and went into the bathroom. Nia sat in a corner, digging through a duffel bag. I smiled at Bella. "Champagne and snacks. I'll be here all night, so feel free to text me or come on down if you need anything, okay?"

"Thanks." Bella's smile was genuine.

"Did you call your folks?" I asked in a gentle tone.

"Tried, got voicemail. I did talk to my fiancé. He's on a work trip in Miami this weekend. I think I might have ruined his night."

Nia looked up, her mouth in an annoying slant. "Oh no, you ruined Ethan's South Beach debauchery! Whatever will he do?"

Bella huffed out a little snort then turned back to me. "Thanks again for being so nice."

I reached out and squeezed her shoulder. Like every other time I'd touched someone here in Cypress Grove, there was no sensation, vision, or memory. It appeared that my psychic powers didn't activate when it came to actual humans.

"Of course, dear." I wanted to fold her into a hug, she looked so forlorn, but didn't because Lauren had come out and was pouring the champagne.

"Night," I said, and walked out.

Someone slammed the door behind me. Sighing, I went down the hall. My eyes landed on the supply closet.

Should I?

Duh. Of course I should.

I leaned in and pressed my ear against the door. There was nothing. Normally I wouldn't be wary. Or afraid. Since the inn had an active and disgruntled ghost until recently, I was extremely suspicious of anything unusual.

Was Billy the petulant teenage ghost back? I sure hoped not. He'd been in some sort of paranormal purgatory when I'd reunited him with his true love. Prior to that, he'd taken to tampering with things like the inn's air conditioner. In August. In Florida.

No, subtle scratching noises weren't Billy's style. He was flashier. Had another troubled spirit taken up residence here? It was exactly what I did not need. Already my face was heating up, which meant a hot flash was imminent.

Taking a deep breath, I turned the knob and pulled open the closet door.

A broom that had been leaning against the back wall teetered. I reached to grab it but flailed in a comical-looking attempt to not knock things off a shelf. The broom fell and smacked me directly on the bridge of my nose.

"Ow!" I cried out as the stiff bristles brushed my eyes. Who stored a broom upright? Me, apparently.

I stumbled back, clutching my stinging face. I wiped a cobweb off my forehead. Gross.

That's when the guests' door flew open. Lauren's blonde head greeted me. For the first time, I noticed she was still wearing the tiara. She held a champagne flute.

"Um, what was that?" she asked in a snotty voice. "Some of us are trying to mourn in peace tonight. Why is your face all red? You should get that checked out."

Now in full-on hot flash mode, I straightened up and smoothed my shirt, trying to appear nonchalant. "Oh, sorry about that. I, uh, opened the closet and a broom fell on me." I rubbed my sore nose.

Lauren arched one perfectly groomed eyebrow. "Riiiight. Well, could you keep it down out here? We're kind of having a moment."

"Of course, my apologies," I said through gritted teeth. Lauren gave me one more withering look before disappearing back into her room.

Walking once more down the hallway, I blew out a breath. This innkeeping thing wasn't for the faint of heart.

Six

Back downstairs, I found Oliver sitting on the sofa, a beer in one hand and his cell in the other. His black-rimmed glasses were off and he was holding his phone a few inches from his face.

He lowered the phone and slipped his glasses back on when I came into the room. "How are they coping with everything upstairs?"

"Hold that thought." Because my face was sweating like a visitor to a theme park in July, I powered into the kitchen, opened the freezer, and took out a little gel ice pack I sometimes used. I swiped it over my face. There. The hot flash had vanished as quickly as it came.

Heaving a sigh, I went back into the living room and plopped down next to Oliver, reaching for my beer. A sip revealed that it had reached room temperature. I didn't have it in me to care and swallowed. Grimacing at the bottle, I shifted my gaze to him. "Bella seems genuinely torn up. Lauren is even more arrogant and is still wearing the tiara. And Nia? I can't figure her out yet."

"Interesting. Well, I got some information from a source."

"A source? Ooh, that sounds like it's full of intrigue. Do tell. Who is the source? Or are you not allowed to say?"

Oliver chuckled softly and shifted so his back was against the armrest. "He's a friend. A local DJ. His mom's the town's medical examiner."

My eyes widened and my jaw dropped. In my old hometown of Sonoma, hot gossip fell into a few categories: what celebrity visited which winery, who was buying a bigger, more expensive mansion, or who had the audacity to drink white zinfandel in public.

Here in Cypress Grove, the scuttlebutt was hyperlocal and juicy. Affairs, breakups, fraught family dynamics, whose witch powers were more powerful, who was better at picking lottery numbers (I was filing *that* information away for future use). Everyone loved gossip. And the women I'd met — Liz the New Age shop owner, Marisol Cross the medium, Oliver's sister Sage — all loved to talk. Apparently, Oliver did as well.

I'd been eagerly soaking up all the local chit-chat, mostly because people in town were so dang unusual and hilarious. Tonight's tidbit was even better because I could learn some local gossip and find out more about Oliver's personal life. And hopefully, about my dead guest.

"I sense there's a story here, my dude."

He opened his mouth to speak, a bashful expression on his face. "Sort of."

I waggled my eyebrows. This was so much better than thinking about what we'd seen at the park. "Spill."

"It's nothing." He paused. "I went out on a couple of dates with the DJ's mom. It wasn't a big deal, and we decided we were better as friends. You know how it goes."

"Hmm." I stifled a smile. It was unclear what was happening between me and Oliver, but something resembling attraction bubbled under the surface. I didn't want to come off as too eager to know the man's dating history just yet — even if I was dying to know. "That's interesting that you knew him before his mother. How did that all come about, anyway?"

"They moved to town a while back. My friend, his name is Calvin Yates but he goes by DJ Ghostwave, is twenty-five. His mom, Lisa, is our age. Divorced. She also has a ten-year-old so Calvin lives with her and helps with his sister. His radio station is at their house here in Cypress Grove, in a garage."

I couldn't imagine having a ten-year-old at this age on top of a demanding job dealing with dead bodies. Any frisson of jealousy I harbored instantly disappeared. "Oh! DJ as in radio, not as in guy-who-spins-records-at-clubs."

"He does that too, but mostly, he runs the local radio, WBOO—"

"Wait. The local radio station's call letters are WBOO?" This made me crack up and snort a little.

"Silly, right? Someone in the 1970s thought it would be cool, and it stuck. Anyway, Calvin is the station manager. He has a nighttime show. Wednesdays through Sundays, from nine p.m. until two a.m. Also..." Oliver's voice trailed off.

"Also what?" I couldn't wait to hear more about DJ Ghostwave and his middle-aged medical examiner mother.

"I'm not sure if I'm supposed to say anything, but I guess I can tell you. It's still a bit of a secret because of local regulations." Oliver's eyes flickered to my mouth. My breath hitched a little.

"You can trust me," I murmured. Goodness, he was sexy in a geeky, silver fox kind of way.

"Calvin also hosts a radio show for the undead."

Record scratch. All lustful thoughts came to a screeching halt. I massaged a knot in the back of my neck and glanced toward the kitchen, where Freddie Purrcury was pawing at his water dish. "Excuse me?"

Even though I'd been in town a few weeks, sometimes the ghostly-witchy-psychic details still stopped me in my tracks.

"Yeah, it probably sounds a little odd to an outsider. He has warlock powers and can communicate with the undead. Three times a week, he does a special broadcast for them. Sometimes more."

I narrowed my eyes. "How do they listen, though? When we saw Billy, he couldn't hear anyone but me, and that's because I was the conduit with my psychometric ability."

Oliver nodded. Billy had been the unsettled spirit that haunted the inn. He'd died in the 1950s. Oliver had helped me research his death and was there when I helped Billy out of ghost limbo. I thought of it as a purgatory of sorts but wasn't sure if that was entirely correct. This place was still a mystery to me, and I suspected it would be for a while.

"Remember when Billy told you he could hear radios from his era?"

I nodded. The ghost had loved Elvis.

"From what I've been able to discern, the undead, well, the ones who aren't fully on the other side and who can reveal themselves to people with certain powers, can hear devices from the era in which they died."

I paused, allowing this to soak in. "Okay..."

"The radio waves transmitted from Calvin's station act like electromagnetic radiation, sending out signals at specific frequencies," Oliver explained, pushing his glasses up his nose. "Those signals can travel through the air and solid objects until they encounter something conductive, like the metal in old radio antennas."

I nodded, trying to grasp the concept, and not wanting to admit to him that I'd never taken physics.

"The radiation induces a current in the conductors," Oliver continued. "That current then vibrates to create the sound we hear from radios. So, for ghosts..."

He paused, meeting my gaze. My face warmed as we locked eyes. Not that long ago, Oliver and I had gone out to dinner. It had been a romantic date, at least until a couple at another table interrupted our conversation about the paranormal and asked for assistance.

I couldn't help but feel that Oliver and I had a connection. Or maybe we didn't, and I had lost all ability to read the intentions of the opposite sex. It was hard to tell after a divorce.

"Being spirits detached from their physical bodies," I squinted, unsure of his theory, "And ghosts still retain some electromagnetic essence from when they were alive?"

"Exactly." Oliver's eyes crinkled with an approving smile. "The radio waves can induce currents in the electromagnetic spirit of a ghost, allowing it to pick up the signal. So Calvin broadcasts to the living and the dead. We can hear his music, and so can the ghosts."

I sat back against the sofa, fascinated but also overwhelmed. The intricacies of the supernatural world here were complex. As an outsider, I had so much to learn.

"But it only works for ghosts from eras when the radio technology matches what they knew, right?" I asked. "Like Billy and the 1950s music he loved."

Oliver nodded. "Additionally, some ghosts can manipulate electricity and electronic devices themselves. They may be able to detect radio waves using trace electromagnetic energy around them."

I shook my head in wonder. Being detached from a physical form gave ghosts certain capabilities? There was an entire ghostly radio listenership out there, apparently.

"Amazing," I murmured. "I had no idea the undead could

interact with radio waves like that. Calvin's broadcasts must provide some comfort and connection. But it makes sense…I think." I chuckled softly. "Well, as much as ghosts listening to the radio can really make sense."

"But this is a long way of explaining what Calvin told me about Megan."

"Oh, right! I'd almost forgotten about the murder. Silly me. What did he say?"

"That Megan was strangled, and that she hadn't been dead for long when we found her. Which we kind of knew, right?"

I nodded and Oliver continued.

"That's all he got out of his mom, anyway. He's trying to find out more. Sometimes Lisa, his mom, is reluctant to tell him things, because he can't keep a secret."

My mouth opened and stayed that way. "So, whoever killed her was on the boardwalk with us?"

Oliver nodded slowly. "Maybe not on our section of the boardwalk, but yes. Unless…"

I leaned in and nodded, prodding him on.

"Unless she was killed by, ah, how should I put this? By something not entirely of this realm."

I was doing a lot of gaping tonight. "You think a ghost killed her? Was that possible? I thought the spirits in town left people alone?"

Oliver pushed out a breath. "The story about Betty the waitress was true."

My hand flew to my throat and I clutched the ruby pendant that my aunt had left me. "Oh dear."

"I wouldn't say a ghost is the number one suspect, but it also can't be ruled out."

"This place gets weirder by the day." I shook my head and glanced around the room nervously, as if a specter might materialize at any moment. I thought of my encounter with the broom upstairs, and a shiver went through me.

Oliver gave me a reassuring smile. "I wouldn't worry too much. Ghosts going on murderous rampages is pretty rare, even around here."

"Well, that's a relief," I said with mock enthusiasm. "Wouldn't want any random poltergeists to suddenly develop homicidal tendencies."

Oliver chuckled. "I think we're safe for now. Besides, if a ghost did kill Megan, it was probably a one-time thing. A vengeful spirit settles a score and then moves on."

I raised an eyebrow. "You seem to know an awful lot about ghostly murder motives."

"Purely academic interest," Oliver replied with a wicked grin.

"Uh-huh." I took a long swig of my warm beer, contemplating this new development.

I set my bottle down and turned to face Oliver on the sofa. "So where does this leave us? Do we tell the cops about the ghost theory or keep it to ourselves?"

Oliver pursed his lips, thinking. "Let's keep it under wraps. No need to make them think we're completely bonkers just yet. Something tells me our new chief isn't thrilled about having to deal with the paranormally inclined."

"My lips are sealed," I said, miming a zipper across my mouth. "But Chief Wolf should've known this came with the territory when he took the job."

Oliver laughed, then glanced at his watch. "Oh wow, I didn't realize how late it was getting. I should probably head out. Man, what a night."

"Of course," I said, trying not to sound too disappointed. My exhaustion had eased and I was getting my second wind. I stood and followed him out of the apartment, through the library, and to the front door.

I opened it for him. The night air was mild and humid. Apparently, this is what passed for fall in Florida.

Oliver stepped outside then turned to face me, the porch light casting a soft glow on his handsome features. "Thanks for the beer. I'll let you know if I hear any more from Calvin."

"Anytime," I said with a smile. We gazed at each other for a moment, the night air suddenly feeling charged between us. Slowly, Oliver leaned in, and I felt myself drawn closer to him. Our lips were just inches apart when a loud yowl sounded from inside the house.

We both jumped back, the spell broken. "Freddie," I said, rolling my eyes with a wry laugh. "Probably he wants treats."

"In a cat's world, an empty dish is a felony," Oliver said, grinning. "I'll see you tomorrow? At the fall festival? I'll be at the Historical Society booth from noon to four."

"Definitely." We shared one last lingering look before he headed down the steps. I watched him disappear into the darkness toward his car, my heart fluttering.

Freddie meowed again from inside. "Yeah, yeah, I'm coming," I called over my shoulder. But my mind remained on that almost-kiss with Oliver, and the tantalizing possibilities of what could have happened.

I closed the door softly and leaned against it for a moment, catching my breath. That near-kiss had left me tingling.

Freddie yowled again, breaking me from my reverie. "Alright dude, I'm getting your food," I called out.

In the kitchen, I filled Freddie's bowl with stinky kibble, my mind still on Oliver. I wondered what was happening between us. Was it attraction, or were we bonding over weird paranormal events?

When I headed back to the living room, I turned to the

radio on the bookshelf. It had been my aunt's and it looked like a relic from the 1940s, an old-style tabletop. The thing was avocado green plastic, in mid-century modern style. The dials and clock display were yellowed with age.

Did this thing work? Only one way to tell. I pressed the "on" button, and the sound of a DJ's deep baritone hit my ears.

"This is DJ Ghostwave, coming at you live from the studios in downtown Cypress Grove. This classic is from the Breakfast Club soundtrack and it's for all you ghosts still haunting your high schools. You're listening to Dead Air with DJ Ghostwave on WBOO. Stay cozy this October, spooks and spirits."

The beginning chords of "Don't You (Forget About Me)" by Simple Minds filled the room, instantly taking me back to high school dances in the 80s. I had a terrible memory for childhood events, but my teenage years were as vivid as yesterday.

I smiled and hummed along, memories flooding my mind. Teased hair, jean jackets, mix tapes from crushes.

Who else in town was listening to this song tonight? Were they alive? Or dead?

The music swelled around me, the soundtrack from my past now drifting through the present. For a moment, time seemed to bend and blur.

The boundaries between this world and the next felt thinner than ever.

Seven

The next morning, my eyes peeled open at five minutes to six. Rain skittered at the windows. It was coming down softly, a mere drizzle, but that wasn't what stirred me awake.

That honor went to Freddie, who was playing his favorite game: Foot Attack.

Normally it was a fun time for both of us, mostly because I could tease and torment him under the safety of a blanket or comforter. This morning, I was on my aunt's sofa and covered in only a thin blanket, which didn't reach my bare feet.

"Ow," I said as Freddie lunged, claws out. Of course, the more I moved, the more he pounced.

"I guess this is my wake-up call," I grumbled as I tried to extricate myself from the blanket, the sofa, and Freddie's murder mittens.

It hadn't been the best night's sleep, for lots of obvious reasons. I yawned and grunted and attempted to stretch the exhaustion out of my middle-aged bones as I made coffee and prepared Freddie's first meal. I scanned the list I'd left on the counter, a rundown of what I was planning to serve for breakfast today.

I'd prepped two trays of cinnamon rolls yesterday and all they needed was to pop into the oven and bake for a bit. That would be a comforting breakfast for the three women upstairs after the horror of last night. I'd dealt with the dough yesterday, and figured I'd make the cream cheese frosting for one tray of the spiral-shaped, cinnamon-filled rolls this morning.

I'd save the second tray for tomorrow. My earlier worries about serving the same thing at breakfast two days in a row seemed silly in the face of, well, *murder*.

I took the rolls out of the fridge so they could rise before baking. I double-checked that the rest of my breakfast spread hadn't been eaten by ghosts. You never knew around here.

Two pounds of locally sourced bacon? Check.

Eggs from my friend Marisol's backyard hens? Check.

White chocolate chip banana bread? Check.

I'd gotten the instructions for the bread from my new trusted recipe source: a local cemetery. I hadn't told my daughter, brother, or mother about this new culinary breakthrough of mine, probably because they would worry that I'd gone mad.

The Enchanted Eternity Park was one of Cypress Grove's biggest tourist attractions. People came from all over to gawk at the intricate granite and marble headstone carvings. They also visited for something else: the recipes.

An entire wing of the cemetery was filled with people whose final wishes were to have their favorite recipe engraved on their tombstone. In my short time here, I'd found some delightful recipes. The delicious snickerdoodle cookies had come from there — they'd been on the tombstone of Janice Dover (1942-2001).

I hoped the banana bread, courtesy of the dearly departed Elsie Wainwright (1903-1999) was also a winner.

While Freddie noshed and the coffee brewed, I peeked at my phone. There was a message from an unknown number, sent at two in the morning.

We're planning on sleeping late today so don't wake us up with homemade breakfast or anything. None of us really eat breakfast.

Since we have to stick around here because of the situation, we're planning on going to that fall festival today. We will eat there in the afternoon.

I heaved a sigh. Why hadn't they told me that during the flurry of emails? I'd asked them specifically what they wanted, and Bella had responded.

I stared at the screen, momentarily annoyed. It must be Lauren. Or Bella. Probably Lauren, though, from the snotty tone that came through loud and clear in the text. Reminding myself that the trio had gone through a lot last night, I looked at my dozen plump rolls. Well, if the guests didn't eat them, surely I would (and Jimbo, Oliver, Liz, and anyone else who dropped by).

As the coffee drizzled into my mug, the machine emitted a disconcerting gurgling sound. I opened the top to check, and a burst of steaming liquid spurted out, scalding my neck.

"Aaaah," I yelped, clapping my hand to my flesh. I swore aloud and Freddie looked up from his bowl.

The coffee maker sputtered pitifully, dripping the last of the coffee onto the hot plate.

Great. Add a busted coffee maker to the list of this weekend's issues. There was no way I could face this morning without coffee.

With a heavy sigh, I checked my neck in the mirror. A red blotch was already blooming, and from the size and shape it looked like I had an epic hickey. Awesome.

It was still a little too warm to wear a turtleneck — I

doubted if it was ever cool enough in Florida to wear one — so I threw on a T-shirt, a light rain jacket and jeans, then grabbed my car keys. I'd have to get my caffeine fix at Ice Ice Baby, my favorite café in town.

The rain had stopped by the time I found a parking spot on Main Street. Inside, the cozy cafe was already bustling with its morning regulars. I ordered an extra-large iced caramel apple latte and a cranberry orange muffin. Feeling revived by the scent of coffee and baked goods, I decided to nosh in the car and take a quick drive past the scene of last night's tragedy.

When I arrived at the parking lot, it was empty. The police tape from last night was gone. It seemed the police had finished their initial investigation of the area.

"Weird," I muttered. It was as if nothing had ever happened here.

I wondered if I was violating some rule or law by being here this early, but the gate was open, so apparently the place was, too. A sign said the park was open from sunup to sundown.

On impulse, I parked and got out of my car. The boardwalk entrance was open. With no one around on this quiet morning, I could retrace my steps from last night and possibly try to make sense of what happened to Megan.

Would my psychometry help in this situation? I intended to find out.

Clutching my coffee for dear life, I started down the wooden path. At least I'd get my steps in today. I'd been sorely lacking in the exercise department since coming to Cypress Grove, mostly because I'd been so busy getting the Crescent Moon in order.

In the soft morning light, the boardwalk seemed peaceful rather than creepy. It was so bucolic and still that I began to wonder whether I'd dreamed the entire horrific event last night.

The air smelled like wet leaves, fresh earth, and the loamy

scent of swamp. A cool-ish breeze rustled through the cypress trees, sending droplets of water pattering onto the wooden planks. Somewhere nearby, a bird let out a morning song, its notes mingling with the chorus of frogs and insects.

The sun was starting to peek through the clouds. Today would be beautiful, a perfect one for a fall festival. I'd been looking forward to the adorably named "Florid-Autumn Fest." It even had a clever slogan: Where Summer Meets Sweater Weather.

The coffee chilled my hands as I walked, its aroma blending with the earthiness of the swamp. Under the board-walk, dark water flowed slowly, its surface shimmering in places where the wan sunlight struck it. Aside from the occasional ripple from some hidden creature, the water was still and smooth as glass.

I was headed in the same direction that we'd gone last night. Since I was walking at a much faster clip today, I soon passed the first spot where Oliver had told his ghost stories.

Perhaps now was the time to test my psychometry. I clasped the wooden railing, which had been sanded to smooth-ness. I ran my hand over the damp surface and closed my eyes.

My aunt's pendant grew warm on my chest. I stood, holding the coffee in one hand and the railing in the other. A tingle shot up my hand, and then I heard noise.

It was as if someone was tuning a car radio quickly, going from station to station without stopping. Snippets of conversa-tion, songs, static, even nature sounds, all competed for promi-nence in my brain.

I lifted my hand and the noise stopped. When I lightly rested it on the rail, the cacophony returned. Hunh.

I took a few steps and touched the railing on the opposite side. Same thing — static with a symphony of voices. For a while I walked and skimmed my fingers over the smooth wood, trying to get a signal. Was I hearing this chaos because so many people had touched the rail?

That seemed to make the most sense, but I'd have to research this later.

Clues to Megan's death weren't coming though, just a riot of noise that was making my head throb. Enough of that. The last thing I needed today was a headache, so I resumed walking.

Within twenty minutes I was at the pond where we'd found Megan's body.

My pulse quickened as I approached the sandy area. The water looked serene and tea-colored today, with a little mist rising in the morning light. I vaguely recalled Oliver saying that some freshwater ponds and lakes in Florida were sepia-toned because of all the tannins in the earth and the swamps.

Today the surface shimmered, almost a coppery hue. A lone ribbon of police tape was still tied to a tree, but other than that, there was no trace of what had happened.

Weird. Chief Wolf and his officers must work fast.

I couldn't shake the image of Megan's lifeless form sprawled facedown near the shore. What had happened during those fateful minutes when she'd left our group? How had she gone back to the fork then walked the other way around — and when did she meet her killer?

For several long minutes I stood on the sand, staring at the water. Was it possible a ghost could commit murder? It seemed silly to me, but after everything I'd seen in a few short weeks here in Cypress Grove, nothing seemed impossible.

It was, however, horrible that something so violent could happen in a place this pretty. I started to walk away but a movement in the pond caught my eye.

The fog. Or was it steam because the water was warmer than the air? I stepped a few paces closer to the edge of the pond. It sure seemed like it was getting foggier.

Groaning because my back felt a little stiff, I squatted. For some reason, I felt an overwhelming urge to touch the water, to feel its coolness on my fingers.

I plunged my hand in, and it was warmer than I expected. The water rippled and swirled around my hand, and I skimmed it through the pond, wondering if there were gators here.

"That coffee looks good. Too bad you didn't bring me one."

The voice was so clear, so girlish, that I lost my balance and almost fell face first into the water. My coffee almost went tumbling and I grabbed it at the last minute, saving my essential morning drink.

"Oh, duck." One knee was soaked, and I scrambled to my feet.

"No ducks in this pond."

"Wh-what?" I whirled around, freaked out that I hadn't seen a soul and now someone was talking as if they were right next to me.

"Your coffee. Is that ice? I don't think I ever tried one of those, because they weren't popular back in my day."

I turned to my left and gasped.

There, standing on the beach next to me, was a ghost.

Eight

I did what any rational woman would do in this situation.

I screamed.

The ghost rolled her eyes in response. That's when I realized that she was young. Around my daughter's age, perhaps younger. Perhaps I was being a bit dramatic. It wasn't like I hadn't seen a ghost in Cypress Grove. Still.

"Oh, no," I whimpered. "Another teenage ghost?"

"I'm nineteen. Practically an adult." She looked me up and down in a gaze reminiscent of my own daughter. Never did I dream I'd go through teenage angst again, but here I was, with the ornery undead.

"Sorry. I'm new here and am still getting used to all of the..." I waved my hand in the air. "Paranormal stuff."

"I can see where it would be a lot for a normie."

I studied the girl. She wore an off-the-shoulder neon pink sweatshirt with matching pink and white striped leggings and white high-top sneakers. Her hair was teased high with bangs and crimped waves, and she had bright blue eye shadow caked on. She looked like she had stepped right out of an 80s aerobics video.

Unlike when I saw Billy at the inn, this ghost was in full color. She seemed to shimmer in the morning light. Beautiful, really, if you didn't think about the reality of it too hard.

"Wow, that outfit takes me back," I said. "Very retro chic. I think I had those leggings back in the day. Capezio? Esprit?"

The ghost girl glanced down at herself and shrugged. "I guess. They were a Christmas gift."

"So..." I began slowly. "Do you mind if I ask what happened to you? Do you live here? Or are you following me?"

"I don't know you. Why would I follow you? And no, I'm not telling you what happened to me. It's none of your business."

I ran my tongue over my top teeth, trying to figure out what I should do next. "So, why are you here now, talking to me?"

"Because you touched the water and apparently, you're one of those who has the special and kinda rare power. It's the only time I can come out of the pond."

This shocked me into silence for a second. "You. Live. In. The. Water?"

"Yeah. A bunch of us do. We all died in the lake. We're all residents of the In Between, though. That's a more global thing."

"Oh my goodness," I whispered, then blew out a breath. This was too strange at this hour. I hadn't even finished my coffee. The *In Between*. That sounded spooky. "How many are there?"

"Let's see." By now we'd begun to stroll the shore, side by side. As if we were pals. "There's Lorena, she died in the thirties. She's like my grandma. Ah, there's a Seminole Indian guy, he's really old. His name is Abiaka. A few have left, and there's a newer guy named Chad. He only came last year."

She paused and obviously didn't see the look of horror on my face because she whispered, "Chad's kind of a dipstick. Totally grody."

I stopped to take a deep breath.

"What? Do you not know what grody means?" She stared at me witheringly.

"I know exactly what that means. I was alive in the 80s. No, I'm shocked that so many dead people are living in a pond." I was practically shouting now. "This is too weird! Why didn't Chad, Abiaka, and Lorena come out when I touched the water? Why you? No offense, but I don't understand."

Again, she shrugged. "People in your realm rarely do. But I think I can totally answer some questions if you stay cool."

"Fine. I'll stay cool. Can we sit for a bit?"

"I rarely get to walk." Her tone was whiny, like a teen.

"Okay." If only I could calm the fear-inspired trembling in my limbs.

We trudged on.

"Okay, so, like, here's the deal: people who are alive, ones with powers like yours, can see me. Other people can't. The ghosts in the water have different abilities than I do. I'm clueless about why I have it, and I don't use it that often. The last time I came up to shore was when a little kid went swimming. Of course, he didn't know he had the power, so I appeared and he thought it was hilarious. That was a pretty cool day, though."

"How long ago was that?" Genuine curiosity was replacing confused horror in my mind.

"Hmm. Let's see. I remember it was the first time I'd heard a radio in what seemed like eternity. I'd been in the In Between for about five years. So, around 1991. Someone had an old boom box. Oh, right! I remember hearing on the radio that Patrick Swayze had been voted as the sexiest man alive by People Magazine. That kind of shocked me."

"Why? You don't like Patrick Swayze?"

"He's like, okay. I didn't have his poster on my wall or anything."

"No? Who did you have on your wall?"

"James Spader." Her girlish grin melted my heart.

"Ah, a woman of excellent taste. You'll be happy to know he aged well."

She looked at me, her button nose wrinkling. "Ugh, I can't imagine him old."

I was about to say *well, we all get there*, but obviously, we all didn't, since she was nineteen and dead. Or living in the In Between. That sobered me up. "Okay, so you only come to the surface if someone with my power touches the water."

"No," she said sharply. "I can come to the surface of the water anytime. I can't come ashore unless someone with your power is standing on the shore and touches the water."

"Ah. Got it."

We walked in silence for a few steps.

"What happens when you come to the surface? Can you see and hear people? Or can you only hear and see me?"

"Sometimes I can see and hear them. Can't talk to them, though. I can only come ashore and communicate with people with your powers, though. I try to stay hidden most days. Sometimes when I'm lonely, I just float along, invisible, and watch everyone having fun. Sometimes that makes me too sad."

"I can imagine. Do you also do this at night?"

Her face lit up and almost sparkled in the sunlight. "Yes! Totally, that's my favorite time, because I can see all sorts of creatures. Like, gators and stuff. Sometimes we all come up to watch the stars and moon, too. It's rad."

That was quite beautiful, but it wasn't what I was getting at. "Did you happen to come up last night?"

"Like, yeah."

"Did you notice anything odd or unusual?" I asked, hoping she had witnessed something related to Megan's death.

The ghost girl paused, regarding me curiously. "I'll tell you, but first you have to do something for me."

I nodded, figuring there would be a catch. "What is it?"

"Bring me a radio. One of those cool boomboxes with the big speakers and cassette deck. Or like one of those clock radios, the kind that looks like a cube. They're totally awesome. I can only hear songs on certain devices. Older ones. I've seen people with newer looking speakers and can't hear anything. I don't know how it all works. But if you play some music for me, I'll tell you what I saw last night. Please? It's the thing I miss the most."

I blinked in surprise. That was an odd request, but simple enough. Or was it? Who had a 1980s radio hanging around? There were several junk shops in town...

"I think I can manage that."

The ghost clapped excitedly. "Oh my god, hella rad! I can't wait."

I had to chuckle at her lingo, which wasn't all that different from my own — me being a Gen Xer and all.

"Okay, it's a deal. But first, can you at least tell me your name?"

She grinned. "It's Tiffany."

"Nice meeting you, Tiffany. I'm Amelia," I said sincerely. "I'll be back as soon as I can so we can chat more."

Tiffany gave me a thumbs up. "Cool beans! Catch you later!"

As I was asking her another question about whether day or night was best for her, she walked back into the shimmering water.

"I should've known you'd come back to poke around. You seem like the nosy type."

This was a different voice. A masculine one. For the second time today, I was startled. I whirled, spilling my coffee.

The cold liquid splashed everywhere, soaking my pantlegs and shoes. I yelped and hopped around, shaking my foot like I was doing some bizarre rain dance.

This time, it wasn't a ghost. It was Chief Wolf, in running gear that showed off his muscular physique in a way that would make Arnold Schwarzenegger himself proud.

His sleeveless shirt revealed muscular arms. His short running shorts highlighted his legs, which looked like tree trunks.

I tried not to stare as I sputtered, "Oh! Chief Wolf, I didn't see you there."

He peered at me through narrowed eyes surrounded by sweat drops. The man obviously took his workouts seriously. I tried not to look at his body, since I suspected he was the kind of dude who noticed when women stared.

No way would I give a guy like him that satisfaction.

His prominent brow furrowed as he looked at the puddle of coffee seeping into the sand. "Making a mess, I see. Were you talking to yourself?"

I hesitated, wondering how to explain conversing with a ghost teenager to Cypress Grove's top cop. How much did he know about the town's paranormal legacy? I wasn't going to be the one to break the news, that was certain.

"Oh, just...you know... enjoying the morning. Trying to get recalibrated after last night."

He nodded slowly, brows furrowed in skepticism. His gaze lingered on the scalded spot on my neck.

"Right. Well, enjoy the morning while you can. I need to question you later today."

"Of course." I tried to project a cool confidence, even though my ankles were soaked in coffee and I'd just had a conversation with a ghost.

"I have an opening at one. Your guests are coming by at eleven-thirty."

I frowned. "You talked with them?"

He nodded once. "I did. Called them right before I came on my run."

One would think my guests would've at least texted me a heads up, but no. "So, the police station at one?"

"The police station at one. Park in the side lot because of the festival. Copy that?"

Apparently, that was his personal catchphrase. Who was I to criticize when I muttered "what the duck" a dozen times a day? "Copy that," I repeated.

I was about to make small talk and tell him that would be perfect since the station is next to the park where the fall festival was being held. But he didn't wait for an answer.

With his jaw set in a line of grim determination, he jogged off.

The inn was empty when I arrived back. The three women were gone and hadn't left a note.

I knocked on Bella's door softly and called her name. No answer. I tried the other room. Nothing. Using the universal key, I softly popped open the door to Bella's room.

No one. For a brief second, I panicked, wondering if they had fled town. My gaze scanned the room. Suitcases and a mountain of clothing were draped over a chair. The tiaras from last night were perched on the nightstand lampshades. The TV was still on, tuned to a reality TV show minus the volume.

Without thinking, I crossed the room to turn it off, suddenly feeling as though I'd been transported five years into the past, when my daughter was about fifteen. She'd leave on TVs, lights, electronics, you name it, all night.

I reached for the remote, which was atop a gold brocade throw pillow on the floor. A strong electric current zapped my fingers. Not the kind of static shock you'd get from wearing rubber-soled shoes.

No, this was the kind of current that made my palm feel like it was being singed. Or branded, like a cow.

"Eesh!" I cried out, then everything went fuzzy. *Oh boy. Here it comes.*

A psychometric vision.

The room in the vision was the same one I'd just entered, but with a different air. The tension was palpable as I saw Nia and Lauren standing close together near the king-sized four-poster bed.

Their eyes were wild, filled with a combination of fear and determination. Bella was nowhere in sight but the sound of the shower running could be heard faintly in the background.

"We've got to tell her," Nia hissed.

"No frickin' way." That was Lauren. Apparently, she had a haughty tone when she talked with everyone, not just me.

"What about the cops?"

"You mean, what about that fine-assed police chief?"

Even in my vision, I winced. Chief Wolf was so not my type, but it didn't shock me that Lauren would find him handsome. She was definitely "thirsty."

"You need to be serious. This is no joke, Lauren. Bella's going to be devastated when she finds out the truth."

The sound of the shower stopped. Lauren and Nia shot each other a warning look.

"Don't say a word." Lauren's tone was too menacing for my liking.

As suddenly as it appeared, the vision faded. My legs felt like licorice ropes, and I swayed a little on my feet. I sank onto the unmade bed, trying to shake out the pain in my head. Sometimes when I had strong visions, they would leave me with a headache. More like a brain ache, actually.

At first it had been scary, and I thought I might be having a stroke. But I was learning to lean into it, and today was no exception. Folding over, I tucked my head between my knees. A few deep breaths helped.

I straightened my spine, my eyes landing on a jar of moisturizer on the nightstand. It was an expensive brand, one I'd longed for years ago but never felt like I deserved to spend that much money on myself.

I reached for it, hoping I'd glean another vision. But nothing happened when I touched the jar.

I set it down, feeling conflicted. This situation posed an ethical dilemma: should I go through the women's belongings, hoping to glean more clues into Megan's death?

Or as the innkeeper, was that unethical?

What were the ethics of psychometry, anyway?

This was a question for Oliver. He was my rational sounding board. I'd ask him later at the festival. Right now, I didn't feel comfortable digging through their stuff. That was the cops' job.

Why hadn't the cops been by to look at Megan's stuff? Maybe that's where the women were: at the police station, with Megan's belongings.

Still, I couldn't shake my nagging feeling as I walked out of the room. I carefully locked the door and walked down the stairs. Freddie was at the bottom. He looked up at me and meowed.

"What's going on, little cat man?" He brushed against my legs, then sauntered over to the Inn's front door and plopped on the indoor welcome mat.

He meowed again. At the same time, there was a knock at the door.

"Anyone there?" A male voice called out. The doorknob rattled, but because I always locked it, whoever was on the other side couldn't get in.

I hadn't been expecting anyone. It took a little getting used to, this innkeeping thing. I wasn't sure if I should leave the door unlocked and open for all to enter, like a regular hotel, or keep it locked like a private residence.

Maybe Helena could answer that. I twisted the lock and opened the door. The creaky sound coming from the hinges made Freddie sprint away. He hated that, and I had to remind myself to either fix it myself or ask Jimbo to do it, since he had handyman skills.

On the other side of the door was a tall, thin young guy with tousled brown hair and a five o'clock shadow standing on the porch. He wore jeans and a wrinkled gray T-shirt. Definitely a millennial hipster.

"Hi," he said in a deep voice. "I'm Ethan. Is my fiancée Bella here? I think she was staying here. The Crescent Moon Inn?"

So, this was Bella's fiancé. I tried not to judge people by appearances, but something about him seemed off. Maybe it was the dark circles under his green eyes, or the tense set of his jaw. He looked like he hadn't slept in days. Poor guy, what with the news of Megan and all.

Probably Bella wanted to cancel the wedding. I would, if I were her.

"Yes, you're in the right place. Nice to meet you, Ethan. I'm Amelia, the owner. I reached out to shake his hand but somehow that startled him. He fumbled, the phone he was holding slipped out of his grasp, and I grabbed it in mid-air.

The moment my fingers touched the cell, a strange tingle shot up my arm. I inhaled a sharp breath as another vision flooded my mind.

I saw Ethan, inside a vehicle. It was nighttime. He was driving and listening to a podcast, a man with a grating voice. The sound of a phone pinging with a text filled the air, and Ethan reached for his phone. Taking his eyes off the road, he glanced at it and smirked.

The emotions radiating from the vision nearly knocked me over—triumph laced with a twinge of fear.

Ethan looked at me oddly and snatched the phone out of my hand. "So where is she?"

"Bella's not here right now, but please come in," I managed. Normally I wasn't one to talk about auras, but whatever was swirling around him seemed slightly off. So much so that I wasn't sure I should tell him where Bella was.

As he stepped inside, his sea glass-hued eyes scanned the lobby. He gave off an intensity I found unsettling. I suspected some women probably found him handsome. But his restless energy put me on edge. And that vision... I couldn't discern what he'd read on the text, but it was a message that had made him feel like he was getting away with something.

"Do you know when she'll be back?" he asked. "She texted me about the, ah, Megan situation. Seemed really upset. Which is understandable."

He scratched the back of his neck, and I noticed his knuckles were swollen and red. Like he'd been in a fight.

"Um. Yeah. I'm not sure when she'll return. I think she and Lauren and Nia are at the fall festival, and they're also scheduled to meet with the police chief," I said slowly. "But you're welcome to wait here if you'd like."

Part of me hoped he'd decline. This man's presence filled me with a vague dread I couldn't quite place. What if Bella was hiding from him for a reason? Or perhaps Lauren and Nia were steering her away from him? The conversation in the vision I'd had upstairs was fresh in my mind.

"Oh, yeah, she told me about all that. Is the festival nearby? Maybe I'll go over there and try to catch up with her."

"Wonderful," I said, a little too enthusiastically, then explained in painstaking, rambling detail, how to get to the festival.

He shot me a slightly confused look but nodded. "I'll probably see you later, when we return. Bella said the cops want her to stay here."

"Okay, sure," I said. "We'll leave the light on for you."

I realized that sounded callous, but I only said it out of sheer nervousness and unease. "I mean, I'm here for all of you. Whatever you need. This is such a difficult time for you and Bella. And Lauren and Nia, of course. I'm sorry about what happened to Megan. It's a real shock."

"Yes. It is." His voice was flat, scarily so. "Well, I guess I'll be going."

He stuffed his hands in his pockets and walked off the porch. I watched him go down the steps, then shut and locked the door. I leaned with my back against it and swallowed hard.

"What the duck?" I whispered.

I took a minute to collect myself, then went into the kitchen. Freddie appeared, of course, because he'd learned that if people were near the big cold box with the food, he'd probably get a second breakfast or a third dinner.

He was right. Still shaken from my encounter with Ethan, I fed Freddie a few tuna treats. Then I washed my hands and checked on the cinnamon rolls. They had risen to perfection and were ready to bake.

Since I'd only had coffee — and had spilled half of it — I figured now was as good a time as any for breakfast. Then again, I was always ready for breakfast food.

After popping the rolls in the oven, I set about making the cream cheese frosting. It was my favorite kind, sweet with a hint of tang. Buttercream was nice and all, but it was a tad too much for my taste.

I added a stick of butter and a brick of cream cheese to my aunt's KitchenAid mixer — thank goodness she had one. My kitchen in California was well appointed, but I hadn't had the chance to move everything here.

As the two ingredients churned together in the mixing bowl, my thoughts did the same. I tried to tally the suspects in Megan's murder. It had to be someone close to her, right?

Bella and Lauren were the most obvious suspects. But would they have had time to return to the entrance and loop around to the pond the other way? It was possible, I suppose, and they would've likely known exactly where Megan was since they all had their cell phones with them.

I'd lost track of them because I'd been having such a good time with Oliver, something I now felt terribly about.

The women in the other bachelorette party, the ones staying at Helena's, weren't suspects in my mind. They had no reason to kill her. Didn't know her. Possibly didn't even talk with her.

But Helena... now she was an interesting person. I stopped the mixer and dipped a spoon into the concoction. It still needed a few minutes; I liked my cream cheese frosting extra smooth. I spotted a lump and sucked in a breath while starting the mixer again.

Helena disliked my aunt and didn't seem to be Liz's biggest fan either. But those two realities didn't lead to her killing one of my guests.

Then there was Ethan, with his intense energy and vague aura of menace. I couldn't shake the strange vision I'd had when we touched hands. What had he been up to last night? He was allegedly in Miami on a work trip. That city was almost five hours away by car, which would explain the deep, dark circles under his eyes.

Or would it?

Come to think of it, Nia's arrival late in the evening was

also odd. She and Lauren were obviously hiding something, from the vision I had upstairs.

I added the vanilla and powdered sugar to the frosting, letting the whisk attachment on the mixer blend it to silky perfection. The cinnamon scent of the rolls in the oven made my stomach rumble.

By now, the frosting was finished. I pulled the beaters from the machine and licked one. I groaned aloud when I tasted it. I could almost bathe in this stuff.

A thought came to me: the performers. They were the only other ones on the boardwalk. But why would they want to kill Megan? Nothing made sense.

Those were the only possible suspects, though. Unless there really was a killer spirit lurking in our midst.

"Please don't let it be a killer ghost," I whispered. "Anything but a killer ghost."

Freddie, who was lingering at my feet, meowed.

Ten

A couple of hours later, after changing into a cute, white T-Shirt, sand-colored capris, white Keds sneakers, and a straw hat, I swiped on some lip gloss and marched the six blocks downtown to the Cypress Grove Police Department. I hoped my crisp outfit would make me feel jaunty and carefree on a day where I was anything but.

The cop shop stuck out like a sore thumb in the quaint downtown. It was exactly one block and across the street from the Astral Attic, Liz's new age supply store on Main Street. The building itself was in the brutalist architecture style, all imposing concrete and sharp angles.

The only reason I knew the style was because of a class I'd taken in college. I'd never understood how anyone would want that kind of visual in a community, and it sure didn't endear me to the police department.

As I was about to pull open the door, the phone in my purse rang.

"Oh duck," I whispered while moving a few steps to the side of the door. I was fifteen minutes early, so perhaps I had time to grab this. Maybe it was a new development in Megan's case.

Wouldn't that be nice...

But, no, it was my mother. I heaved a sigh and answered. "Hey there, I'm a little busy."

"You move to Florida and you ignore your mother. Just great."

"Mom."

"It's like you've forgotten I exist."

"Mom."

"You don't even know what's going on with your own daughter."

"What?" I shrieked. "What's wrong with Jenny? What happened?"

Mom lived in Arizona, about an hour from Jenny's college campus. Despite my difficulties communicating with my dear mother, the two of them were thick as thieves. I was relieved when Jenny decided to attend school there. At least if something happened, family would be nearby.

"She's got a boyfriend. And she's going to his house for Christmas. Can you believe it?"

I leaned against the rough concrete and shut my eyes. "I know, Mom. Jenny told me last week. I'm flying to California for Thanksgiving and she'll have dinner with me there. Then she's going to New Mexico for Christmas and then Las Vegas for New Year's."

"Oh, so you were keeping this from me. What has gotten into you? How can you let your twenty-year-old daughter roam the streets like that?" Mom continued to berate me. "Jenny's turning twenty-one in two months. What about Chad? Where will he be for Thanksgiving? Have you thought that far ahead?"

I turned so I was facing the wall and banged my forehead

softly against the concrete twice. The holidays were the last thing on my mind.

"I don't know where my ex-husband will be on Turkey Day." Hopefully carving off an appendage with the electric knife. "Nor do I care."

"Well, you don't have to get snippy. I thought perhaps you'd all have a final holiday together." Mom had always been Chad's biggest fan, even after the cheating. Said he would eventually "come around."

Yeah, right.

"Nothing would be worse than dining with my ex-husband."

"Well. And what about me and my husband? Where will we go?"

My mother felt that everything in the family must revolve around her. Since my divorce, I'd tolerated less of this kind of behavior.

"I assumed you'd want to hang out with your friends in Arizona. You did last year."

She sputtered for a few seconds, then I cut her off.

"I'm a little busy right now. Something happened with one of my guests and I need to chat with the police chief."

"What happened? Was there a theft at the hotel? Or, no, it must have been a slip and fall. Those old stairs. What's the insurance policy like? Why are you even bothering with that old, ratty place?"

As I was about to answer, the station door opened, almost thwacking me in the nose.

"Sorry," I called out.

Three women emerged: Lauren, Nia, and Bella.

"Hey," Bella said brightly, then saw I was on the phone and mouthed, SORRY.

"Hi," I said. "You all okay?"

Lauren rolled her eyes and grabbed onto Bella's arm, pulling her along without acknowledging me. So rude and weird. Jeez louise.

"Amelia? Are you there? Can you hear me?"

I clenched my free hand into a fist. Something about my mother made me feel like a teenager. "Let me explain later, okay? I gotta run."

I hung up and went inside. The interior of the building wasn't any cozier than the exterior. My sneakers made soft thwap-thwap-thwap sounds on the terrazzo floor. I reached the window and told the receptionist I was here for the chief.

She looked at her computer, then at me. "He's waiting for you. I'll buzz you in, and it's down the hall and to the right."

I nodded and followed her instructions. When I reached his office, I knocked on the open door.

"Enter," he commanded.

I fought back an eye roll. Did this man have to be so stiff and formal at all times?

"Have a seat." He gestured to a worn chair on the other side of his desk.

While taking my hat off and plopping onto the seat, I glanced around the small space. Dark wood paneling straight out of the 1970s covered the walls, contrasting with the bright Florida sunlight streaming through the blinds.

Framed photos of muscular police dogs covered nearly every inch of the wall behind the desk. I recalled my various conversations with Sage and Liz about the rumor around town that the chief was a werewolf.

I'd always scoffed at the idea, but the photos of the dogs were giving me pause.

"What a good-looking animal," I remarked, pointing at a framed desk photo of a giant, brown-and-white dog. "Is it your personal pet?"

"I used to teach classes on K-9 training at the FBI Academy in Quantico."

"Oh, well that makes sense."

He squinted. "What does?"

I sat for a second, stumped. It made sense to me in the context of the werewolf rumors. But I wasn't going to tell him that. "All the dog photos, of course."

He grunted in response and stared at me sternly from behind his large oak desk.

I tried not to squirm in my seat, but it was difficult. He had a way of making me feel like I was guilty for merely existing. This didn't jive with my post-divorce self. I'd seemingly lost my patience with men lately.

"Before we begin, what's that on your neck there?" he asked gruffly.

I tapped my neck with my fingers. "It's not a hickey, if that's what you're implying."

"That wasn't on my mind." He did not look amused by my tepid attempt at humor.

"Oh! Well. My coffee maker malfunctioned this morning and scalded my skin."

The Chief raised one dark eyebrow. "Not a scratch? From the victim, perhaps?"

"No, absolutely not," I insisted. What was he implying, anyway? "It was hot coffee, that's all."

"And the red mark on your forehead?"

I frowned, touching my temple.

"No, in between your eyebrows."

I let out a laugh. "Oh, I was chatting with my mother on the phone just before coming inside. I banged my head against the building like this."

I pantomimed by moving my head forward and back. Probably I looked like I was pretending to rock out at a heavy metal concert. He stared at me in horror.

"It didn't hurt, I was merely a little frustrated. I just tapped my forehead, nothing serious. You know, mothers. They can be a lot." A pause. He totally didn't grasp my humor, probably because at our essence, we were like oil and water. "Just joking."

An awkward silence settled in the air while he stared at me. Then he shook his head and jotted something in his notebook.

I pasted on a smile while he wrote. He cleared his throat then leaned back in his chair. The wood creaked under his beefy frame.

"Alrighty then, let's get started with your statement about last night."

He began questioning me about the events leading up to Megan's death. I recounted everything as accurately as I could, starting from when I was at the inn with Liz. All the while I worried that the Chief suspected me of wrongdoing.

Why else would he fixate on the stupid coffee burn? I had to stay focused and not let him rattle me.

"Obviously, my men talked with you last night, but I wanted to hear some of the answers directly from the horse's mouth, so to speak." He eyeballed me.

He looked so stern, so much like my ex-husband in that moment, that two emotions swelled inside me.

Annoyance and the deep, dark desire to ridicule. For five seconds, I fought mightily not to let either show. I lost.

"Are you calling me a horse? Do you expect me to neigh?" I cracked.

My absurd joke was met with a stone-faced glare. "This isn't funny, Ms. Matthews. What was your relationship with the victim? Did you know her well or have any conflicts with her?"

I shook my head. "I'd only just met her and the other

women when they arrived at my inn a few hours before the incident. We didn't have any kind of relationship or conflicts. I'd never even talked to her until yesterday. Lauren did all of the arrangements with our inn via email."

The chief scribbled some notes. "Can you account for your whereabouts and actions throughout the entire haunted swamp walk last night?"

"Absolutely. I was with Oliver. Er, my friend Oliver Everhart, the town historian, the whole time. We walked together and talked. I never left his side."

Chief Wolf's pen paused over his notebook. "You didn't separate from the group at any point?"

"Well, we were at the head of the group, so yes, we were a bit separate." I wondered if he questioned Oliver like this. I was about to ask but decided to be on my best behavior.

He scratched his chin thoughtfully. "Alright. You mentioned finding the body. Did you touch or move it at all before calling for help?"

I shook my head adamantly. "Of course not, I'd never do that. Oliver and I found her at the same time, since we were together. As soon as we realized she was dead, Oliver and I were shocked, of course. We tried to keep the others away until help came."

He leaned forward. The weight of his stare made me nervous, and when I got nervous lately, hot flashes would usually follow. Sitting in front of a police chief with a sweaty pink face wasn't the best look.

"Has anything else unusual happened in the last day or so?"

I glanced around helplessly, trying not to laugh. Unusual was also known as "Tuesday" in Cypress Grove. I let out a cough. "You wouldn't happen to have water, would you?"

With a grunt, he hoisted himself out of his chair and went

to a cube-shaped fridge in the corner. He extracted a tiny bottle of water that almost disappeared in his big hands. He gave it to me and I sucked it down while he resumed his place behind the desk.

I quickly told him about Nia's late arrival and how she looked muddy. Of course, I included the part about her car breaking down. Then I explained that Ethan had showed up this morning, looking disheveled. I considered whether to tell him about the vision in the guest room, or what I'd felt during my brief encounter with Ethan's phone, but I didn't get the impression the Chief was interested in the metaphysical.

"I'm not sure if their late arrivals mean anything, though. They're basically kids. You know how it was when we were in our mid-twenties."

"No, how was it?"

I blew out a faint breath. This man didn't seem to want to find common ground with me, even in casual conversation. "You know, working hard. Partying hard. When you're that age, you don't know which way is up. Time doesn't have the same meaning."

He grunted and nodded. "Anything else?"

Helena's taut, pretty face popped into my mind, as did her statement about Wolf being a terrible lover. How could I probe this issue without offending him? I couldn't.

And yet I was terribly curious how a rough-and-tumble guy like him ended up with her. Frankly, he didn't seem her type, and vice-versa.

"Well, there's Helena, of course," I said, running my fingers over the brim of my cute straw hat.

"What about her?" His eyes flashed.

Hmm. That was some reaction. *The plot thickens.*

"Well, she apparently left the group and went to her car. I didn't see her slip away, didn't know she left until your guys brought her to the beach in that ATV thing. But I'm sure you chatted with her, given that the two of you have a history."

"A history?" He raised one bushy eyebrow.

"She told me that the two of you..." The words died in my mouth because he was staring at me with an expression that could melt ice. Eep.

"We went out to dinner once, right when I arrived in town, because the Realtor who sold me my condo here in town is a mutual friend. That's all." He was back to grinding his molars.

Hmm. That didn't sound quite as juicy. *The plot thinnens.*

He sighed. "Alright, let's switch gears for a minute. Tell me about yourself, Ms. Matthews. What's your story? How'd you end up here in Cypress Grove?"

I pressed my lips tight together, surprised by the personal questions — and a bit shocked he wasn't impressed with my information about the two people who arrived late. "Well, I'm originally from California. I used to own a cookie company there. But after my divorce, I was looking for a change. My aunt left me the Crescent Moon Inn, so here I am."

Probably best not to get into the many weird details that happened upon my arrival here. It was entirely possible he'd already heard them, since folks around town liked to gossip. Something told me the chief wasn't cool with rumors, though.

He wrote a few notes, then looked up. "And what's your marital status currently?"

I shifted in my seat, confused why he needed to know this. "Divorced."

"Single mother?"

"Yes, I have a daughter away at college."

We talked for a few minutes about the University of Arizona and how he once went to K-9 training in the Grand Canyon National Park.

He scratched his chin. "Okay, let's move this along. Word

around town is you claim to have psychic abilities. Something called 'psychometry?' Care to explain? Also, do you make any money from your, ah, talent?"

I blinked in surprise. The town gossip network had reached him! "I don't *claim* anything. But it's true, since arriving here, I've discovered I can sometimes see visions of past events by touching objects. It's been alarming, to say the least, especially since I didn't believe in any of this prior to moving here. And no, I'm not monetizing my psychic power."

Chief Wolf leaned back, regarding me with a smirk. I couldn't really blame him for his skepticism, since I'd also been a non-believer until a few weeks ago. Heck, I wasn't even sure how much I believed even now.

"Hmm, copy that. Well, here's some advice. Don't go poking around in this case using any 'powers.' This is a police matter, and I don't want civilians interfering. Let us handle it. Understood? We're the professionals, even in a town filled with so-called fortune tellers."

"Of course, Chief. I would never get involved in the investigation." I smiled politely, hoping this line of questioning was over.

But that was a lie, wasn't it? I fully planned on procuring a radio for Tiffany the ghost, in hopes she could give me a clue. But it wasn't illegal to chat with a ghost, was it?

A quick glance at Wolf's expression told me it wasn't the right time to ask and he'd probably say yes, ghost sources were off limits.

We chatted for a few more minutes about being newcomers to town. As a gesture of goodwill, I told him about the amazing chicken salad at the Haunted Hearth.

"It's close to my friend Liz Lopez's store, the Astral Attic. You should check out that place. Even if you're not into psychic stuff. She has some beautiful gifts there."

Oddly, that seemed to resonate, because his expression softened. He reached for a small dog figurine and gave it a death grip. I was worried it would break in his hand, but then I realized it was one of those stress-squeeze things. I also recognized that it wasn't a dog.

It was a wolf in mid-howl.

"Thanks for the tips," he said. "I guess we're about done here."

I raked my bottom lip against my teeth. I was dying to know the answer to one question. Well, duck it. I was going to ask.

"Chief, do you have any leads or suspects yet in Megan's murder?"

Wolf's expression instantly hardened. I could almost hear the molars grinding.

"That information is need-to-know only," he growled. "And please, don't suggest I visit one of the town's many psychics, or tap into your powers or whatever they are. And don't offer up one of your visions. I rely on science and good, old-fashioned police work. Copy that?"

It had been a wise move not to tell him about my vision in the guest room. I held up my hands in a placating gesture. "Sorry, I was just curious if you'd made any progress."

"It hasn't even been twenty-four hours. Don't worry your pretty little head about it," Wolf snapped. "My team and I have everything under control."

His condescending tone made the hair on the back of my neck rise, kind of like Freddie when he spotted a squirrel out the window and felt the urge to attack. I bit my tongue to avoid firing back with a fabulously sarcastic retort.

After an awkward silence, Chief Wolf stood abruptly.

"We're done here. Remember what I said. Don't go poking your nose where it doesn't belong. This is police business. And potentially dangerous, since we have a killer in town. I'll contact you if we need anything further."

He ushered me out of his office, his large frame looming over me. He walked me all the way to the building's front door and gestured to the lot out front.

"You know, if you'd like to park here and go over to the festival, feel free. No one's using those spaces today."

"Oh. I walked but thank you. That's a nice offer."

He nodded and went back inside. Hunh. What an odd gesture of kindness from a grumpy man.

As I stepped outside into the mild Florida fall day, I resolved to do some sleuthing of my own. I had my own ways of getting information, and I wouldn't let Wolf intimidate me — or psych me out with offers of free parking.

I needed two things: another coffee, and more clues. Hopefully I'd find at least one at the nearby fall festival, but both would sure be welcome.

Eleven

The Florid-Autumn Fest was held in Bicentennial Square, a lovely, expansive grassy knoll with a gazebo smack in the middle of downtown. It took up two entire city blocks. Liz and Oliver were somewhere in the crowd, and it was going to take me a while to find them. Probably I should just text, but I also wanted to wander a bit alone.

Today, the place was jammed with people, many of whom were wearing sweaters, boots, and scarves despite the pleasant, seventy-degree weather. Families and other folks strolled around eating candy apples, drinking cider, and perusing artisans' cute booths. Before last night, I couldn't wait to poke around and buy some gifts for my daughter, Jenny. We'd planned on exchanging gifts over Thanksgiving.

Now, my mind was scattered. I felt out of focus. Shopping under these circumstances didn't seem right. Neither did socializing or being festive.

It was always the perfect time for coffee, though, and I let out a breath of relief when I saw the Ice Ice Baby food truck.

There was a line, but I didn't mind. It would give me a few minutes to collect my thoughts.

I stood at the back of the queue, tapping my foot to the upbeat Taylor Swift song playing from the truck's speakers. Jenny loved this song, and I snapped a photo for her. I also sent a quick text to Liz and Oliver, saying that I'd come find them as soon as I grabbed coffee — and asked whether they wanted anything.

They didn't, so I slipped the phone back in my bag.

The aroma of coffee and fried dough wafted through the air, making my mouth water. I adored local festivals like this and was thrilled to know my adopted home had a packed calendar of community events. My old town of Sonoma had lots of happenings as well, but the place had been so inundated with tourists that most things had been difficult for locals to enjoy.

In my book, Cypress Grove was like the equivalent of Goldilocks finding the perfect bowl of porridge. It was just right.

Ahead of me were two women who looked strangely familiar. As I studied them, I realized we were all wearing virtually the same outfit — white shirts, tan capri pants, and white sneakers.

The only difference was that I had on a hat. I chuckled to myself. It must be the unofficial middle-aged woman uniform.

As the line inched forward, I decided to strike up a conversation with the women. "Well don't we look like triplets!" I said with a laugh.

The women turned and looked me up and down, then chortled as they realized we had on matching outfits.

"Oh my gosh, you're so right!" said the blonde. "We're style sisters."

We chatted as we stood in line. Turned out they were

friends, nurses at the local hospital, and they hadn't anticipated they'd be in the same clothes. We talked about the festival (this was the twenty-fifth year), about the coffee truck offerings (we all decided on the caramel mocha apple), and who had the best, most decadent dessert booth (the deep-fried Oreos were the obvious winner). It felt good to have a lighthearted moment after the stress of the murder investigation.

As we were inching forward, an older guy holding an expensive-looking camera approached. His clothes were threadbare and his Teva sandals were held together with creatively applied duct tape. How odd. I averted my eyes from his feet, since his toenails looked like corn chips.

"Excuse me, ladies. I'm Gregg Russell from the local paper. You three look so cute in your matching outfits. Do you mind if I get a quick photo?"

"Not at all!" said the blonde. She put her arm around the brunette and me.

"Alright, say 'sisters from another mister!'" Gregg called out.

We did, and erupted in giggles as he snapped a few photos.

"These are great, thanks so much!" Gregg took out a pen and a notebook. "Mind if I get your names?"

He handed the notebook to the blonde, who carefully wrote her name down. The brunette did, as well. They were next in line and the barista called for them, and we said our goodbyes as the brunette handed me the pad and pen.

I quickly scrawled my name, not wanting to hold up everyone else in case a spot at the food truck window came open. When I was done, the photographer took the pad from me and glanced at it.

"Amelia Matthews? The new owner of the Crescent Moon Inn?"

"That's me."

"I saw your name in the police report online this morning," he said, his voice a touch too loud.

The two women I'd just been joking with turned to listen.

"Police report?" I replied softly, not wanting to cause a scene. I tugged at my earlobe, realizing I hadn't put in earrings today.

"You found the body of that tourist near the pond. Man, I wanted to work on that story today but my editor sent me here. He put the new kid on the murder. Say, how about you give me an exclusive interview?"

My face froze in a mask of horror. This was a dilemma. I wanted to flee from this reporter. I also wanted coffee.

"No comment," I finally said.

"Someone's going to knock on your door and ask you to do an interview," Gregg said. "You might as well talk to me."

"I'm not really in the right headspace. I'm sorry."

He reached in his back pocket and pulled out a frayed wallet, the woven rainbow kind that hippies used to carry. "Here's my card. Honestly, though, if you're so broken up about the murder, what are you doing here at a fall festival, joking and laughing?"

I took the card while gaping at him, unsure of what to say. By now the two women I'd chatted with were standing next to us, listening.

"Gregg, that is so rude," the blonde said.

"Yeah, she's probably still in shock. Hon, here, have my coffee. You deserve it. I'm sorry you're involved in all that murder business."

Before I could tell her that I hadn't chosen to be involved with anything murder-related, the brunette thrust a massive cup into my hands. "It's the caramel mocha apple. I'll have a sip of my friend's. They're so huge anyway, I can't drink the entire thing."

"Thanks." I shot her a grateful smile, trying to pretend that Gregg didn't exist. That felt rude, though, something I absolutely hated.

"What do I owe you?" I asked the woman.

She waved me off and wandered away.

"Thank you. Superwomen don't always wear capes," I called out. Hopefully Gregg would get the message and scram.

"Hey, lady! Can you please move along if you're not going to order? Some of us need our caffeine," a guy in line called out.

Ugh. I was messing everything up. Shaking my head, I started to walk away, but Gregg ran ahead and stood in front of me. He pressed his palms together in a prayer gesture.

"Please? I need this interview. I need a win. It's difficult being the oldest guy in the newsroom. All you need to do is give me a few quotes about what you saw, and how you felt. It won't take long, I promise."

As much as I sympathized with his plight about age discrimination, I didn't think it was the best idea to talk to a reporter. "I'm sorry, I'm not up to that." I took a step.

"Did your psychometry lead you to any clues?"

His question cut straight into my heart. I whirled around. "Excuse me? How did you know I have psychometry? I've only been in town a few weeks."

"I have my sources," Gregg said vaguely. "Word gets around in a small place like this."

I studied him for a moment. His wrinkled clothes, the way he seemed desperate for a story. Nothing added up. But it rarely did in Cypress Grove. I shook my head. "I don't think my ability has any relevance to this tragedy. The police are handling the investigation. You should talk to Chief Wolf."

"Like he'd tell me anything," Gregg scoffed. "I know you've been looking into this case yourself. Don't try to deny it."

What? How could he possibly know that?

"I have no idea what you're talking about," I said evenly.

"Please. I have sources, remember? People in this town talk." Gregg gave me a knowing look. "You were at the pond today, from what I hear."

The only one who knew I was there was Chief Wolf. Was he Gregg's source? Anything was possible in this town.

Gregg lifted a bushy eyebrow. "Help me out here, and I'll keep your extracurricular investigating between us and out of the paper."

I hesitated, feeling trapped. Gregg was blackmailing me, in not so many words. But I couldn't let him deter me from finding answers about Megan's death. Was there a way to give Gregg a statement and possibly gain new information in the process? I pondered this for a second.

"Amelia, there you are! I've been looking all over for you."

Oliver had suddenly appeared at my side, a veritable knight in shining armor. Okay, he was in jeans and a zip-up blue hoodie that made his eyes look dreamy. Whatever. He was out of breath, as if he'd been running. His dark hair was adorably rumpled and his glasses were slightly askew.

He grinned at me and put his hand on the small of my back. "The Historical Society booth is right over there. C'mon. And Gregg, please. Have some mercy. Amelia's been through a lot."

"Lady, think about it, and call me, okay? Don't throw away my card," Gregg shouted, a look of wild excitement in his eyes. "Wait. Oliver, you were at the scene, too! How about you and me sit down for an interview? The three of us! My treat for coffee!"

Shaking his head, Oliver propelled me out of Gregg's orbit and into the crowd.

"Thanks for saving me," I said.

"I spotted what was happening from a mile away. Gregg's well known around town. He's a pest but he's also a good guy, deep down. You looked quite uncomfortable, and I'm sorry that happened."

"I was uncomfortable. I'll tell you about the entire conversation when we get somewhere quieter."

Oliver glanced at me with concern. "What happened to your neck?"

I explained about the coffee maker mishap as we wound our way through the crowds. The Historical Society booth was clear on the other side of the park, which wasn't as busy. Probably because there was no food or drinks. When we arrived, I spotted Liz.

"Oh my goodness, you made it! I was thinking about calling an attorney for you." She folded me into a hug, wrapping me briefly in a cloud of patchouli and coconut scents.

"What did you think was going on?"

She lifted her shoulders into a shrug. "That the chief was arresting you on false accusations. I don't know. You never know with cops, even ones as handsome as Christopher Wolf. This case is too weird and my intuition tells me that it's very complicated."

Liz was one of the few in town who didn't have psychic powers. But she was taking grimoire classes. I'd recently discovered that a grimoire was kind of like a recipe book for spells.

"No, my conversation with the chief was strange, but didn't end in arrest. I can confirm that he has a lot of photos of dogs on his walls and desk, though." I shot her a knowing look, and she shot one right back.

Oliver chuckled and shook his head. "I'm sure he's not a werewolf."

I wanted to put a stop to this conversational black hole, knowing it would lead to lots of speculation and silliness.

While I normally loved that kind of thing, today I needed to remain focused.

Liz sidled up to me. "What's that?" She pointed at my coffee burn. "Have you been making out like a teenager? Is that a hickey?"

I practically spit out my coffee. Oliver's cheeks flushed pink and he turned away.

"No. Coffee maker injury." I bit back a grin.

"Mm-hmm," she responded.

Wanting to get off the topic of me making out with Oliver, and since there seemed to be a lull in the crowds in this part of the festival, I spent the next several minutes telling them about everything that had happened today. I used sweeping gestures and a bit of humor. The vision I'd seen in Bella's room. My encounter with Ethan. The chief's interview. How Gregg the reporter harangued me.

"Wow, that's a lot for one day. It's not even three p.m." Liz let out a low whistle.

I cracked a lopsided grin. "Wait, I'm not finished. I didn't even get to the ghost who came out of the water."

Their eyes grew wider with each word.

"Man, you really do have a powerful ability." Oliver shook his head. "What I wouldn't give for that."

"Right?" Liz said. "She's one-in-a-million."

By now, another member of the Historical Society had joined us at the booth. His name was Johan, and he was a professor at Oliver's college.

"He's taking over for me while I do a talk on the side stage about the park's history," Oliver explained. "You're free to hang out here, or come with me, or—"

"Or join me shopping." Liz threaded her arm through mine. "This one needs to de-stress."

"Sounds good to me." We began to walk off.

"Wait, Amelia?"

Liz and I stopped, and somehow, she whispered without moving her mouth, "I think he's going to ask you out."

Grinning, I stepped away from her and toward Oliver. "What's up?"

"I was thinking about Tiffany the ghost and the radio. My DJ friend can probably help. Do you want to go meet him tonight?"

"I'd love to, but what about the guests? Should I leave them alone? Normally I'd say that I could, but this isn't a normal weekend."

Oliver tapped his index finger to his lips. "Wait, I've got it. Let's ask Sage. Or Jimbo. Or both. Sage said her plans for a steak and bake were canceled. Maybe they can hang out at the inn while we go out. I'll text them."

"You are a lifesaver. Thank you. Wait. Steak and bake?"

"There's a guy in town that grills steaks and bakes potatoes in his backyard, and everyone eats around a pit fire and tells stories."

I nodded. That sounded wonderfully weird. "Oh."

"Pick you up at eight?"

I nodded and rejoined Liz.

"A second date?" She waggled her eyebrows. Just days ago, I'd had dinner with him. Liz had been eager to hear every juicy detail, but there had been none to share.

"Not exactly." I tried and failed to fight back a smile. "We're going to visit a DJ. Hopefully he can give me a radio for Tiffany."

She nodded. "Guess it beats the last date I went on."

"I cad some really awful dates after my divorce. There was this one guy, though..." I visibly shuddered.

"That bad, huh? Was he our age?"

"Yep."

"Let me guess: he was looking for a nurse or a purse?"

A laugh bubbled up from my belly. "Both? He had been divorced only a month, told me he'd already been dating, and mostly prettier and thinner women than me. Then asked if I had health insurance. How about you?"

"Oh no," she mock-screamed. "I can sum up my last bad date in two words."

She pulled me to a stop under a palm tree and looked deep into my eyes. Liz thrived on being theatrical and I loved listening to her stories unfold.

"What are the two words?" I asked.

"Truck balls."

I paused, unsure of what she was saying. "Like those... obscene things that hang off the rear bumper of a truck? Truck nutz? Nutz with a z?"

She nodded slowly. "He showed them to me while picking me up for dinner. Really started the night off on the wrong foot. Er, nut."

I was laughing so hard that tears came to my eyes. "But how was the rest of the date?"

"He ordered lobster and conveniently forgot his wallet."

We continued on, laughing the entire way while telling bad dating stories. When we got to the end row of booths, we turned and our laughter quieted. Shopping was serious business.

Most of the booths had a new age or spiritual theme. One sold healing crystals and offered tarot readings, while another sold incense and meditation CDs. Further down, a woman demonstrated reiki techniques as ambient music softly wafted in the air.

Handmade jewelry incorporating runes and astrological symbols adorned another table. Dreamcatchers swayed lightly in the autumn breeze above a booth stocked with books about traditions from Florida's indigenous tribes. We paused at every stall.

"There's so much cute stuff," I gushed while checking out a tye-dyed, white-and-pale-blue cotton T-shirt that said, "CYPRESS GROVE: Psychic Capital of the World."

I bought two. One for me as a show of pride in my new hometown, and one for Jenny. Then Liz and I wandered to the next booth. A sparkly, hand-painted sign read, "Potion Commotion: For the Modern Witch."

"Ooh, let's go in here. I know the owner. And maybe we can find something to help us understand men," Liz joked.

"I'll pass, thanks," I snarked.

Still, the stuff in the booth seemed intriguing. I picked up a small bottle labeled "Menopause Magic" and showed it to Liz.

"Will that make someone disappear when hot flashes hit? Because if so, I'll take a case of it," she joked.

The booth owner, an older woman with flowing gray hair, a gauzy peach dress, and bangles up her arms, came over to me, smiling.

"Ah, the Menopause Magic! A popular tincture. One spoonful, and it'll cool you down faster than you can say, 'Where's my hand fan?'" Then she spotted my friend. "Oh! Liz darling!"

She and Liz embraced. She introduced herself as Leah, and I soon discovered they'd known each other casually for years. She apparently bought all of her herbs from Liz.

While Leah talked about her potions, Chief Wolf himself walked by the booth. He looked more than a little flustered, as if he was searching for someone. In his police uniform, he also stood out among the many women in tye-dye and linen hippie outfits.

Our eyes met.

"Hey there," I said. "You looking for me?"

"No," he said brusquely.

"This works on men, too," the booth owner said while eyeing Wolf. Liz unfurled a feral grin. She was incorrigible.

"Chief Wolf, interested in some Menopause Magic? Might help your investigation a bit," Liz joked, holding the bottle in the air.

His eyes widened and his jaw worked back and forth. He scowled. "I think I'll stick to good old-fashioned police work, but thanks for the offer, ma'am."

He stalked off.

"That man needs to relax," Liz said. "He's too good looking to be that uptight."

Odd. I wonder why he was here. One would have thought he'd mention attending the festival when we talked about it earlier. I turned back to the potions.

Leah launched into a long explanation about what was in the bottles. She and Liz started to chat about herbs and the inventory of Liz's shop. As they talked, I reached for another bottle, a sample. It had the words "Harmony Tincture" written in cursive on a cheap label. I unscrewed the cap and lifted it to my nose. It was a pleasant smell, similar to vanilla but with a crisp apple base note. I did the same with the "Love Potion #5."

"Harmony Tincture brings happiness to all those who consume it," the woman said. Liz nodded along. "And if you have any powers or abilities, my potions will enhance them! They can be used like any flavoring extracts in recipes, by the way."

I was taking a big sniff of the Love Potion — it smelled alluring and yummy, like a rich, expensive cinnamon — when I spotted a familiar face in the distance. It was Wolf, and he was looking grumpier than five minutes before. On the verge of angry, really. He was also gesturing in a forceful way, but I couldn't see who he was speaking with.

I reached into my purse and took out two twenties, handing them to the booth owner. "We'll take both the menopause and the harmony stuff. Sorry to have to run. Liz, I think our attention is needed elsewhere on last night's matter."

The woman started to prepare a paper bag with twine handles, but I grabbed the two bottles and stuffed them into the outer pocket of my purse. We said goodbye, and I pulled Liz to the side, in between booths.

"Chief Wolf is still here," I whispered. "And he looks pretty angry. Let's see what's up."

"Ooh, surveillance. Love it. Which way?"

"To the left. Kind of by the bike racks near the sidewalk."

Trying to act nonchalant, we walked from between the booths and took a hard left.

"I think I see him," Liz muttered. "C'mon. He's on the move."

It wasn't difficult to spot Wolf, since he was so tall and the only person in sight in a cop uniform. He was walking toward the police station.

"Let's speed up a little."

Liz and I power walked until we were away from the crowd and practically on the street. We stopped when we had a clear view of Wolf.

"Holy cannoli," Liz said. "Look who he's with."

Walking alongside the chief was none other than Helena.

"Don't stare at them," Liz said. "Pretend you're not looking."

We made a big show of peering at a flyer for the Monster Mash Fun Run 5K as we watched them stroll away.

"Like we'll ever run a 5K," Liz snorted under her breath.

"He's walking her to her car," I whispered. "Is that weird?"

Once they disappeared from sight, Liz and I looked at each other.

"I'm sure he's filling her in on the case. Or something. Maybe they're friends," I said weakly. It didn't square with his fury when I mentioned their date.

Liz shook her head. "I don't trust anything that woman's involved with. And since you told me she went out with the chief, well, that's quite disturbing on many levels. Also disappointing, since I figured he had better taste than her."

Twelve

"I think we need something stronger than coffee for this," Liz said. "I know just the place. C'mon."

While I followed Liz through the festival throngs, I pondered the significance of seeing Wolf and Helena together. Helena clearly unsettled and concerned Liz, which in turn bothered me. I hadn't known Liz long, but we'd bonded. I trusted her opinion.

We stopped at a booth sporting a big sign that said, "BOOZY MILKSHAKES," and despite the fact that it was still light out, I decided to indulge in a treat. Okay, a second or third treat. To me, this fell under the category of self-care.

The rich, velvety pumpkin pie shake coated my tongue as Liz and I strolled through the festival. The boozy whipped vodka cream on top added a delicious kick that instantly lifted my spirits. Nothing like a spiked milkshake on a sunny fall day.

"I wish Marisol was here to try this," Liz said, taking a long sip of her shake.

Marisol Cross was another woman I'd met since coming to town. She was a bit older. Of my new friends, she was the one with the most psychic abilities. Not only was she an accomplished medium, but she was also a tea witch.

I'd never heard that phrase before, but I'd come to find out that Marisol specialized in something called Tea Magick, which meant she worked spells into herbal tisanes.

"How's she doing, anyway? Have you heard from her?" I asked. "How's the reunion? Any word about the high school sweetheart?"

Marisol was at her fiftieth high school reunion, up in Brooklyn. She'd been nervous because her high school crush was going to be there, and he was single. As was she. They'd been chatting on Facebook for months.

"They hit it off and are supposed to have brunch today. Apparently, he owns some eco-tourism company in the Dominican Republic, in his parents' hometown."

Marisol was also of Dominican descent. "Wow, that's pretty cool."

We chatted about Marisol's prospects of a second chance at love while we perused the racks of a designer that offered pretty dip-dyed cotton skirts.

"Hey, cowpokes!" The familiar voice was followed by Sage's tawny hair and signature cowboy hat. "Fancy meetin' you two here. Hey, what's up with your neck? Oh, I know what happened!"

Sage winked.

"It's not a hickey," I said. "My coffee maker spurted hot water on me."

"Sure," Liz teased, and I swatted her arm.

Sage's face fell. "Ouch, I thought it was a curling iron burn. I get those all the time."

She, too, was drinking a boozy shake, the orange cream leaving a faint mustache on her upper lip. "You two staying out of trouble?" she asked.

Liz snorted. "With Amelia around, trouble follows her like a fart in yoga pants. We've been sleuthing."

"Cool beans," Sage said. It both mystified and amused me that my new friends were so seemingly chill about murder investigations. She took another sip and swallowed. "Listen. I meant to tell you. Speaking of stinky business, did I mention what Bella and Lauren said about Megan?"

"No," Liz and I practically shouted in tandem. We pulled Sage out of the clothing booth and over to a picnic table where we plunked down.

Sage slurped the remnants of her drink and swallowed. "I heard them talking about Megan last night, after she left the group. Before she was found dead, of course. Bella and Lauren said Megan's been a total drag lately, like she was asking for something bad to happen."

"When did you hear that?" I asked. "At what point in the night?"

Sage shook her head. "It was after the zombie and before the mummy."

"That would have been in between stations one and two. Hmm."

"That's super sketchy. Definitely makes my spidey senses tingle about their involvement in this whole mess." Liz drummed her fingers on the wooden table.

We continued dishing about the case, the strange happenings around town, and how Cypress Grove's energy had shifted since the bridal party's arrival.

"Don't you feel the subtle shift?" Liz asked.

"I do," Sage replied.

They both looked at me. "Just because I have psychometry doesn't mean I can feel the energy in the air. I didn't notice a thing."

While Sage and Liz chatted about the aura over town, I checked my messages. Oliver had texted.

Just finished with my talk. BTW, Sage says she's all set for tonight.

I looked up. "Thanks for coming over to stay with the guests."

"Hey, no problem. I was going to see if Jimbo wanted to join me. Let's go ask him."

"He's here?" For some reason I thought Jimbo was at the inn today. Eep. The guests all had codes to get into the main door of the Crescent Moon, and they had the run of the place. Was it okay to allow people to roam around the inn while I was gone?

This was something I hadn't thought through. What could the bridesmaids steal, though? Georgina the gator?

"Yeah, he's working a booth. C'mon."

The three of us hoisted ourselves out of the picnic table and walked toward the middle of the festival, where most of the crowd was gathered near a platform and a bluegrass band.

"There he is," Sage cried. She seemed to be quite excited to spot Jimbo.

Liz and I burst out laughing when we saw where she was pointing.

Jimbo stood at a booth that advertised "HUG A FLORIDA MAN."

"Pose with an actual Floridian and a baby gator," it said in smaller letters.

The foot-long alligator wore a tiny Florida flag bandana around its neck. Jimbo held it gently as he posed with a beaming woman. Bless this wonderfully weird town.

"Who wants a hug," Jimbo called out. "I know you do, Sage."

Liz and I watched as she and Jimbo cuddled close and took selfies.

"They seem pretty chummy," Liz observed. "Maybe there's another kind of energy over Cypress Grove, hmm?"

"What energy would that be?" I asked.

"Love and romance."

"I dunno about that," I mumbled. But my mind was definitely on tonight, and the handsome historian who would accompany me in my sleuthing.

Any desire I held in my heart dried up as soon as I arrived at the Crescent Moon and found Lauren poking around the library. She was dangerously close to the heavy tome that activated the sliding bookshelf, the secret door that led to the apartment.

"Well, hey there, can I help you?" I tried to keep my tone friendly and even.

Lauren shot me an icy glare that could freeze lava. "I'm just looking around. This old place is interesting but could use some updates."

I tensed, uneasy about her snooping after the vision I'd had upstairs. Seeing her also made me feel guilty about poking around in their room. And Ethan—was he here right now?

"Did Ethan find Bella? He came by earlier and said he would catch up with you all at the festival." I asked lightly.

Lauren smirked. "Oh yeah, he found her all right. They're having alone time upstairs, if you know what I mean. I've been kicked out and am staying in Nia's room now. In the bed that was for Megan. Creepy, right? No need to move me, though. Nia doesn't want to sleep in a room alone."

My stomach knotted. Something was definitely amiss with the four of them, but I wasn't sure what. I searched for a friendly olive branch, in hopes of getting Lauren to open up. "Hey, want to bake cookies with me? I picked up an interesting ingredient at the festival."

"Ew, no. I've had enough sugar this weekend to last me a lifetime." Lauren's nose wrinkled in disgust. "I'm going back upstairs."

She shuffled out of the room. Goodness.

I escaped to the kitchen in my aunt's apartment. I refrained from eating one of the rolls, wanting to save them for Jimbo and Sage, who would make short work of them tonight.

I preheated the oven, and checked on Freddie. He was snoozing on the bed, seemingly annoyed that I'd woken him.

A sigh escaped my mouth. This was a tough crowd around here.

After slipping on my apron — I'd bought a new one in town and it had a cartoon woman wrestling a gator with the words "DO ONE THING EVERY DAY THAT SCARES YOU" — I got to work on my baking, in hopes of relieving some of the stress swirling around.

Gemma Hilliard's Pretzel Surprise Cookies was another recipe I'd found at the cemetery, and this might be just the thing to relax my overactive mind.

As I melted the butter with brown sugar, I tried not to dwell on Megan's unsolved homicide. Of course, when one tried not to think of something, it was impossible to do anything but.

The air was filled with a rich, caramel aroma. I whipped an egg, watching glossy ribbons fold into the melted mixture.

Sure, Megan was a downer, from what little I saw. She also had made questionable choices, if her friends were correct. But none of that added up to murder.

The steady beat of the spoon against the bowl soothed me as I added flour, rolled oats, and chocolate chips. Then I added the two ingredients that drew me to the recipe in the first place.

Pretzels, and maraschino cherries.

The trio of sweet cherries, salty pretzels, and gooey chocolate was too good to pass up. Once the mixture was well combined, I took a teaspoon and scooped some out of the bowl, making sure I had every key flavor in the sample.

I popped the entire thing in my mouth. "Dang," I whispered through my mouthful.

These were going to be tasty.

Freddie appeared in the kitchen door, probably thinking I was calling him for Tuna Time.

"Ooh, I almost forgot," I said. "The tincture. Thanks for reminding me, Fred."

He purred loudly as I wiped my hands on the apron and went for my purse on the kitchen table. I reached into the side pocket for the bottles and yelped.

"Yow! What the..." I pulled out a broken shard of glass. "Oh, no!"

One of the bottles had broken. Gingerly I plucked glass out of the pocket. Liquid had seeped through the inner pocket lining and soaked the label of the remaining, intact bottle.

I brought it a few inches from my face. Which bottle had this been? The Harmony Tincture was in the white bottle... no, that was the menopause stuff. Or... oh, heck, I wasn't sure.

Either way, I decided I'd still add the potion to the cookies. Whether the effect was harmony or an easing of perimenopause symptoms, I was on board. Still, I figured I'd split the batch and put the tincture only in half the mix.

I scooped rounds of dough onto the sheet pan, admiring their bumpy, imperfect surfaces. The oven's heat buffeted my cheeks when I opened it to slide the pans inside. The first batch didn't contain the potion, the second did.

While the cookies baked, the knots in my stomach loosened. I ran through the case suspects—Bella, Ethan, Lauren, Nia. Who was hiding something? The cookies' sweet scent grew stronger, making my mouth water.

As the second batch baked, I grabbed a still warm cookie from the first. Sea salt would be perfect so I sprinkled a few grains atop the cookie then took a bite.

Tart cherry pockets contrasted with melty chocolate. Yessssss.

Gemma Hilliard had written an excellent cookie recipe, rest her soul.

Thirteen

A couple of hours later, Oliver, Liz, and Jimbo arrived at the inn. I was still covered in flour, since I'd also experimented with some cheddar-chive biscuits. They hadn't come out as perfect as the cookies, but they were still quite tasty.

"Sorry! I've been baking. Cookies and stuff. Come on into the apartment." I waved them inside.

I led the trio through the lobby and the library, through the hidden bookcase door, and into my aunt's apartment. I still thought of it as hers, even though I planned to eventually live in the space. Freddie had already claimed it as his own, and was sprawled on the back of the sofa, like a chunky orange tiger.

Part of me wondered if he was so comfortable with the apartment because he was communicating with Aunt Shirley in some way. I'd noticed that he was meowing at the closet at one point but was too busy to investigate. Around these parts, I had to pick and choose my sleuthing.

Murder always took precedence.

"Smells good in here," Jimbo said. He was carrying an orchid plant. "Amelia, this is for you."

"Another one? Thank you." I accepted the plant, admiring its fragrant pink flowers. "It's more gorgeous than the last! I'll take any and all orchids. This one will go in here."

We all trouped into the small kitchen, where I set the orchid on a windowsill. I quickly explained that I'd made two batches of cookies and pointed at a silver tray piled high with the treats. "This one contains some of that tincture I bought at the festival. Now, I'm not sure if this is menopause tincture or harmony. There was a little mishap with the bottles. But I figured I'd see how, or if, the stuff works. The other plate," I gestured to a large, red ceramic platter with near-identical cookies, "Are plain, with no tincture. Feel free to try any, or all."

"Good deal," Jimbo said, rubbing his hands together.

"Who doesn't need more cookies in their lives?" Sage said.

"And if the guests want any, please explain that one has the tincture in it. I don't want to be accused of surreptitiously drugging them or something. Who knows if the tinctures even work? I stress bake, and that's why I made everything when I got home. In fact, let's just leave this batch of cookies here on the counter. But don't forget the biscuits. There's no tincture in those."

I didn't want to say that I busied myself with baking because I was so nervous about the guests — and Ethan — upstairs. They'd been silent as ghosts for hours, which was unsettling. I'd even thought of ways I could knock on their doors to find out if everything was okay, but every excuse seemed hollow and intrusive.

Maybe I was starting to feel the vibe around town that Liz had mentioned. Or the aura. Or the whatever. But something felt off, and had since I'd returned from the festival. Truth be told, I was thrilled to be getting out tonight, and not just because I'd be spending time with Oliver.

The trio stared at me. "I'll go change, be ready in three

shakes of a lamb's tail," I said, then scurried into the bedroom where I kept my weekend bag.

I quickly threw on a hunter green, long-sleeved cotton dress and a pair of white Keds. After strapping my trusty fanny pack around my waist, I fluffed my hair and applied some lip gloss.

There had been a time in my life when I adored red lipstick, but these days, regular lipstick didn't love me. It feathered and seeped into the subtle lines around my mouth, reminding me of my grandma.

Aging wasn't for the weak. Or the vain.

Still, a quick check in the mirror revealed that I didn't look so terrible, especially considering the circumstances of the last day. "Not bad for someone dealing with murder and ghosts," I whispered to my reflection while straightening my fanny pack, er, belt bag.

I walked out to find Sage and Jimbo on the sofa, already watching TV.

Oliver was halfway through a biscuit. "I couldn't help it," he said between bites. "It's incredible. I like how you baked in the cheese."

When he finished, we said goodbye to Jimbo and Sage — who were by now absorbed into an old Western on TV, natu-rally — and climbed into Oliver's car.

"Calvin—"

"DJ Ghostwave," I chimed in, just because I wanted to say the guy's full stage name.

"Yes. DJ Ghostwave. Calvin Yates. There are a couple of details you should know."

This ought to be good. "Okay?"

"For one, he only wears bowling shirts. The louder and wilder the better. And two, he loves weird food combinations. So don't be alarmed, especially since your palate is refined."

I snorted. "I'm not so sure about that."

"Well, just be prepared. Last time I was there he ate a tuna fish and gummy bear sandwich."

"I'll try to overlook any culinary horrors, thanks."

We took a few turns into a neighborhood next to my own while I filled Oliver in on how I'd seen the chief and Helena together at the festival.

"Interesting," Oliver drawled. "He seems like a by-the-book cop. But it's Florida, so corruption and a lack of ethics isn't uncommon in law enforcement. I wonder what's up with Wolf, though? Could he be protecting Helena for some reason?"

I was curious as well, and stared out the window, deep in my thoughts. The street was filled with cute bungalows and small Mediterranean revival homes. Since it was October, many of the properties sported Halloween decorations. We parked in front of a bungalow and got out of the car.

"This way," Oliver said, gesturing with his head toward a home with a giant inflatable spider covering an entire window.

As we approached the small, white bungalow, I could hear the thumping bass of electronic dance music emanating from the garage out back.

We followed a stone path along the side of the house, passing an overgrown garden filled with herbs and flowers. The scent of jasmine hung heavy in the night air. Through a back window I could see an older, gray-haired woman cooking in the kitchen, swaying to the music as she chopped vegetables. She looked sensuous and relaxed, and I was immediately envious.

I stopped. "Is this okay to be traipsing around this property? Who is that?"

"That's Calvin's mom," Oliver whispered.

Oh, the woman he dated...

"Should we say hello?"

At that moment, a man in his thirties with a beard joined the woman. "Is that her son?"

The man sensually clasped her jaw in his hands, and the two kissed deeply. I gasped, clutching a strand of invisible pearls. "What the duck? I hope that's not her son."

Oliver chuckled and put his hand on the small of my back, guiding me further into the yard. "That's her new boyfriend."

"Oh! Well, then. Maybe Liz is right. Maybe love *is* in the air," I muttered.

"What?" Oliver asked.

"What?" I said, pretending not to understand his question.

I didn't bother elaborating because by now we could see the detached garage, which looked more like a barn. The door was pulled aside, revealing a young man inside a makeshift studio.

Towering speakers and a mixing board took up most of the space, with vinyl records stacked to the ceiling along one wall. There was a library-style ladder propped against the shelves.

Black light posters depicting aliens and ghosts covered the others. One of those twenty-foot-high skeletons from Home Depot loomed in the corner, its toothy grin greeting us.

There was also a disco ball.

Calvin had his back to us as he transitioned between songs, headphones on and white bowling shirt bedazzled with blue rhinestones sparkling under purple lights. He turned and broke into a grin when he saw us.

"Oliver, my man!" He grabbed Oliver in a quick bro hug, not missing a beat on the turntables. He was a handsome kid. "And you must be Amelia. Heard you've got a situation on your hands. Hang on, I need to go on air."

He turned and fiddled with something on the sound board and spoke into a microphone that looked like it was cobbled together from spare parts. "This is DJ Ghostwave, coming at you live from Cypress Grove, Florida. We're the spookiest radio station in the psychic capital of the world. Tonight, it's seventy degrees and the vibe around town is...complicated."

He laughed, and something about the sound made the hair on my arms stand up. Not because it was ominous, but more in a *holy-crap-I'm-living-a-wild-adventure* kind of way. Just a couple of months ago my entire day was made if I found a parking space at Trader Joe's. Now I was seeking clues about a homicide from a Gen Z DJ with an afro who broadcast to the living and the undead.

Calvin continued. "It's now time to transition out of our electronic lounge to our hella popular eighties night. For all of you ghosts and goblins getting your spooky on, this one's for you."

The rising sound of The Specials' "Ghost Town" filled the air. Calvin took off his headphones.

"Excellent tune," I said. "Haven't heard this in years."

I noticed a plate of food sitting on a wooden barstool parked near the console. Was that peanut butter and crackers, piled high with mini marshmallows and pickle chips? Oh dear. My nose crinkled involuntarily.

"Yeah, we thought you could help us with a dilemma. Amelia's got a ghost who wants to trade information for a vintage radio." Oliver jammed his hands into his jeans pockets. He said this like it was the most normal thing in the world. As if we were asking a neighbor for a cup of sugar.

I snort-laughed a little, then corrected myself into a cough.

Calvin didn't miss a beat. "Okay, I gotchu. Did she say what kind of radio?"

"Eighties-era. A tape player, a boom box, maybe one of those Sony Dream Machines. Remember those? They looked like white cubes?" I pantomimed holding a small box.

Calvin, who was probably no older than twenty-five, stared at me blankly. Of course he wouldn't remember them.

"I loved mine," Oliver said. "I thought it was so cool and modern. Like the height of technology. I'd tune into Art Bell's Coast to Coast on AM radio and listen to it all night. Freak myself out with all the UFO reports."

"A great show. Man, I've listened to some old episodes on YouTube," Calvin said. "C'mon. I think I have what you need. First, let me cue up a few more tunes and launch the auto play."

He tapped a few buttons on the console, then instructed us to follow him deeper into the garage studio, near the giant skeleton. Along the back wall was a tall, gray metal cabinet. He twisted the handle, revealing shelves of electronic equipment from every era.

A few cords tumbled out, and he easily caught them in mid-air.

"Let's see. Eighties. Hmm." He pulled out a boom box with rounded edges. It was a vibrant purple.

"No, I think that's more 90s. We didn't have CDs in the early to mid 80s." I tapped the circular disc player atop the device.

"No cap," Calvin said.

I knew from my daughter that 'no cap' was something The Youths said. I wasn't sure what it meant, so I nodded along with a sage expression. So did Oliver. Our eyes met, and I knew what he was thinking.

No cap made no sense.

"Here we go, fam." Calvin grunted as he shuffled a few things around. "Okay, hold this."

He shoved a vintage wooden radio into Oliver's arms, then reached deep into the bowels of the cabinet.

"Sony... Dream... Machine. Oof." He pulled out a familiar white cube.

I applauded.

"This one runs on batteries, too," Calvin said, a hint of triumph in his voice. "I rewired the whole thing so it could be portable. Sweet, right?"

"You're a genius, man," Oliver said.

"Let's make sure it works." Calvin walked over to a long table that was covered in electronic parts in varying states of repair. He moved aside a speaker and fiddled with the Dream Machine. "We should probably dust it off, too."

Static gave way to the sound of a radio being tuned from station to station, which reminded me of when I was touching the boardwalk rail earlier this morning. I shivered.

"Are you cold?" Oliver touched my shoulder. "I think I have a jacket in the car. I can grab it."

"No, I'm fine, thanks." We exchanged little smiles and my stomach fluttered.

"So, does this information trade with the ghost have anything to do with the woman who died there last night?" Calvin asked as he wiped the little radio with a yellow chamois cloth.

"It does," Oliver said.

"She said she saw something at the time Megan, er, the victim, died." I paused. "The woman who was killed was a guest at my inn."

Calvin stopped wiping. "Bummer. I'm sorry."

"Thanks. We're trying to get to the bottom of it."

"Have you heard anything from your... sources?" Oliver asked.

"You mean, my mom?" Calvin chuckled and shook his head. "She won't tell me anything. No matter how much I ask. And trust me, I asked. Whenever something like this happens, something unexplained, I like to keep certain folks in town up to date with news, if you know what I mean."

Was he talking about ghosts? I looked around, uneasy. My eyes landed again on the sandwich with the marshmallows and pickles.

Calvin didn't seem to notice. "My mom won't tell me any details on this one. Says it's confidential information. Here you go."

He handed Oliver the radio and I thanked him. I'd have to bake something special for him.

"Anytime. Anything for my man Oliver." He glanced at the sound board and I sensed he wanted to get back to his tunes.

"We won't keep you, but I wanted to ask a question. Okay, maybe two." I looked up, into Calvin's large brown eyes. He sure was tall.

"Go for it."

"Do you know anything about the chief? Christopher Wolf?"

Calvin tilted his head. "Like what?"

"Is he ethical? Corrupt? Professional? What's he like?"

He shrugged. "Dunno. I try to stay away from cops at all costs. My mom might know, and I'd normally tell you to go inside and ask her. She'd probably be willing to dish the dirt, but she's on a hot date tonight."

He glanced at Oliver, probably checking to see if the detail about his mom affected him. But Oliver's attention was on a vintage, space-age radio sitting on the table. He fiddled with a knob.

"No worries, bro." It was the first time I'd used the word *bro* in conversation, and it sounded clunky and ridiculous. Gah. Regardless, I jumped in with my next question. "Why do you think Tiffany, the ghost, wants the radio so badly? This is the second spirit I've met who loves music. What's up with that?"

The corner of Calvin's mouth quirked up. "Many ghosts just want to listen to something other than the quiet of the In Between. Others, it's a comfort thing, hearing a familiar sound from their era. Either way, it's good to help them. It sometimes can push them along to the next realm. Which is what they want. To move on."

He made a shoo motion with his hands as if he was flicking away something unwanted. "You know, Ram Dass said, 'we're all just walking each other home.' When you give the spirit her radio, think of it like that."

My jaw dropped at the sudden philosophical, surreal twist in the conversation. I felt like I'd just landed in a Salvador Dali painting.

"Uh, well, okay, that sorta makes sense," I mumbled, even though it didn't. "I guess we'll be going now."

"Hey man, thanks. We'll come say hi another time. Appreciate you." Oliver clapped him on the shoulder, breaking the weird, mystical vibe that all but swirled in the air.

"Song's about to end," Calvin yelped, racing over to the board. "If you see your ghost tonight and bring the radio, tune in to 88.5 FM. That's the special station for the In Between. She might not know about it, and I'm trying to get the word out. So, tell her, okay? And tell anyone you meet from the In Between. I'm playing some righteous tunes from the 80s tonight. Oh, here's some flyers, give them out to any spirits you see."

He reached for a stack of brochures and handed it to me.

Sick of the same old terrestrial radio stations? Want something a little more out of this world? Then tune your dial to 88.5 FM for paranormal playlists handpicked by DJ Ghostwave... spinning live from downtown Cypress Grove...

"Thanks." I imagined myself handing them out to a crowd of appreciative ghosts. "Wait. Can I hear 88.5? Or is it only for the In Between? Sorry for all the questions."

"There are no stupid questions, bro." Calvin grinned. "If you've got powers, you can hear the station. Simple as that. But let's find out."

He tapped on the sound board and "Bela Lugosi's Dead," by Bauhaus filled the air, then turned the volume down and asked Oliver for the radio back. The barn was unsettling in the silence.

We watched as he flipped the radio on and tuned it to a station. The Bauhaus song wafted from the tiny Dream Machine speaker.

"Can you hear that?" he asked me.

I nodded.

"Oliver? You?"

Oliver shook his head.

"You got the power," Calvin said, handing me the radio. I flipped it off.

Now that all my questions were answered — well, the pressing ones, anyway — we thanked him again and left. As we were walking to the car, Oliver asked, "Did we just get roped into doing some street marketing to the undead for DJ Ghostwave?"

He grinned and opened my door for me while I playfully slapped him on the chest with the brochures.

"I think we did."

<h1 style="text-align:center">Fourteen</h1>

I didn't even have to tell Oliver where to go next. He knew to point his car in the direction of the Marigold Wentworth Cypress Boardwalk Trail.

As I was about to ask him our odds of being arrested if we were caught skulking around in the dark, my phone rang. A chill went through me when I saw the name.

Jenny

My daughter was twenty. She never made a phone call unless it was a dire emergency.

"Oh God, oh God," I mumbled, my heart in my throat as I tapped the screen. "Jenny! What's wrong?"

"Mom, I'm okay. Calm down. I wanted to call you before Gramma did."

My heart felt like it was filling the inside of my body, throbbing with anxiety. "What happened?"

"Gramma and I were in an accident. But we're okay! We're not in the hospital or anything."

"A fender bender. Don't be dramatic." The dismissive voice in the background was unmistakably my mother's.

I let out a long, exasperated sigh. This did not seem like a crisis, although my heart was still thumping a mile a minute. "What happened?"

"Well, Gramma picked me up from the dorm to go shopping, and I was driving us to the mall in my car when we were at a stop sign. We were behind a car."

"No, we were behind a truck. A big truck. The kind with the giant tires. I think they race on TV." My mother's voice was loud and clear. They were on speaker.

"It wasn't a monster truck, Grammy. So anyway, Mom, the truck started to back up like it didn't see us. I used the honk button and the guy wouldn't stop."

"Wait, wait, wait. The honk button?" I asked.

"The horn," Mom chimed in, obviously annoyed. "Your daughter doesn't know the word for horn."

I glanced at Oliver, who was trying not to laugh.

"How did I raise a child who doesn't know the word for horn?" I said to him. "Gen Z, man. They're something else."

"Whatever. Anyway, we're fine, the car's fender is super destroyed, and we just wanted to tell you so you're not shocked. We're not hurt, Gramma charmed the truck driver by flirting—"

"I did not, missy! Dear, the food's here, let's eat, I'm famished," my mother called out.

"Okay, gotta go, Mom, you might be getting an email from the insurance company. Love you and Freddie. Bye."

"But... wha..." I shook my head. There was no use in calling Jenny back and explaining that the insurance paperwork needed to go to her father since he paid that bill.

"This," I waved the cell in the air, "Is a Monday problem."

"Everything okay?" Oliver's smooth, low voice snapped me back to the situation at hand: that I was in a car with a man who not only was polite and handsome but smelled good too.

Oh, and that ghost hunting thing.

"Yeah, mom stuff. My daughter and mother got into a little crash in Arizona. They're fine. All good. Okay, let's chat about what we're doing at the park. What are our odds of getting arrested?"

Oliver tilted his head back and forth, as if he was pondering. "The odds are not zero, but I'm pretty confident in our ability to talk our way out of it, if we're caught."

"I'll take that."

By now we were at the entrance to the Cypress Boardwalk Trail. We drove in silence as we rolled to a stop in the parking lot. We were the only car in the large, eerie lot, which was illuminated by a lone streetlamp that looked like it belonged in a noir film.

We climbed out of the car. An uncanny stillness hung ominously in the air. I thought about how excited I'd been when I drove in here last night — and how devastated I was to see Megan, lying on the sand. A shudder went through me at the memory.

Oliver rummaged around his trunk and handed me a flashlight. He carefully wrapped the Sony Dream Machine in a towel, then slipped it and a water bottle into a small backpack. He slung it around his shoulder.

"Thanks for the flashlight," I said, the sound of my voice swallowed by the night. I clicked it a few times, testing the beam.

Not even the drone of cicadas or the croak of frogs could be heard. We started out on the trail and I inhaled a sharp breath as our flashlight beams bounced off the cypress tree trunks.

"This seems creepier than the other night. Doesn't it?"

I half expected Oliver to tease me or call me a wuss. That's what my ex-husband would've done in this situation, which never failed to annoy me. Actually, my ex would've never been brave enough to do this at all. He would've thought this entire situation, from my psychic powers to how I was seeking information on a homicide from a ghost, a ridiculous waste of time.

"Yeah, I think it's because we're alone and not with a larger group. It's okay, though. You've got a big, strong, professor to protect you." He shot me an adorable smile. "Seriously, we're okay. I'm not worried about the undead here. The living... well, that remains to be seen. But something tells me that we're not dealing with a random killer. Also, I've got pepper spray."

I hoped he was correct. And I hoped his pepper spray was in working order.

An opaque mist drifted between the cypress knees, muffling all sound. It was as if the very air was holding its breath. The temperature was chilly, yet wet and humid. It was a creepy and uncomfortable feeling, similar to those peri-menopausal hot flashes where your insides felt like they were on fire, but your skin was cold and clammy.

The only illumination came from a sliver of moon over-head. The wooden planks creaked under our feet as we ventured out over the inky water. All around us rose the slender cypress trees, their knobby knees jutting up from the murky swamp like arthritic fingers. Spanish moss hung in shrouds from the branches, swaying slightly in an unfelt breeze.

Every small sound was amplified in the stillness. The gentle lap of water against the pilings, the rustle of unseen creatures scurrying through the undergrowth. A loud splash made me yelp.

"Here, take my hand," Oliver said in a raspy tone.

I didn't hesitate to take him up on that offer, but it had nothing to do with my budding attraction to him. Now, I needed comfort.

I gripped his palm in my right hand, sweeping my flashlight

beam through the mist with my left. Shadows undulated and shifted, my imagination turning them into lurking, threatening figures.

"Wait, what's that?" Oliver squeezed my hand and we came to a stop. I braced myself for an alligator. Or worse.

But it was totally innocent.

There, near one of the boardwalk railing posts, was a thin slip of an object. He aimed his beam of light on it.

"A leaf?" I asked.

We got closer. "Oh, it's just a piece of trash, nevermind," he said.

Something about it made the pendant around my neck ice-cold and I reached for his arm. "Wait."

I let go of Oliver's hand and bent over to pick up the object. "Dang, my back," I whispered, feeling a twinge in my lower spine. Ignoring the sensation — it had been there since I was pregnant some twenty years ago — I scooped up the trash and unfolded it.

"It's a piece of paper. No, a business card. Whoa," I said a little too loud, my voice slicing through the stillness.

Oliver peered over my shoulder. "Does that say…"

"Jessa Purcell, performer, actor, musician, magician," I whispered. My fingers began to tingle. "Oliv…"

I couldn't get his name out before my vision started to swim. The last thing I felt before the vision was the wooden railing under my hand. I held on for dear life.

I was on this boardwalk, but there are a lot of people around. It's in another part of the trail, though, on one of the turnouts and not the main path. All but one is in costume. Oh, it's the performers. The mummy, the vampire, the creepy clown, along with several others from last night.

And Megan.

"Hey, do you have another one of those?" she asks.

"*Sure, here you go.*" *The woman, who is dressed like a vampire, hands her a cigarette and lights it.* "*How's your night going?*"

Megan takes a deep drag and shrugs. "*You all were the best part of the night. Bachelorette weekends are stupid. Especially when you hate the bride but are obligated to be in the bridal party because of family. You all were cool, though.*"

I listen as she asks about whether they do local theater, and the actors answer. As they're talking, they watch a woman jog by.

It's Helena, and she only half glances their way. The group continues to talk while the performers put props in bags.

"*Let me give you my card. My name's Jessa,*" *the vampire says.*

Megan accepts it with a thanks and slips it into her pocket. "*I'm going to head out. You guys need a hand with all that?*"

"*Nah, we're good,*" *Jessa the vampire says.*

"*I'm going to find a bathroom. Have a good one.*" *Megan walks off.*

In the vision, it's as if I'm following Megan from the air. We walk at a fast clip back to the entrance. She goes for the visitor center and tries to pull open the women's bathroom door. When it doesn't open, she swears aloud.

"*Guess I can't get in there,*" *she mumbles.*

She rummages around in her pocket and pulls out a phone, tapping on the screen.

"*Heyyyy,*" *she says in a sing-song voice.* "*What are you doing?*"

There's a pause and she laughs. "*Ethan, that's so mean! But it's why I love you. How long until you get in town... ooh you're not that far. An hour? I can't wait to see you. I'm at this stupid park. You should meet us here. Wouldn't that be wild? I know, we'll be almost done by the time you get into town.*"

I gasp, but of course she doesn't hear me. Ethan? The groom? I thought he was in Miami on a work trip. What's going on?

"You know what I'm going to do? I'm going to surprise them and pretend I'm dead. Really mess with their night. I'm going around the other way and will meet them at some stupid pond. I was going to put some fake blood on my face but the stupid bathroom's closed at this park and I don't want to do it in the dark. Oh, I've got it. Maybe I'll wrap my scarf around my neck like I've been strangled."

She cackles then says, "I love you."

"Oh no, poor Bella. Her fiancé is sleeping with her bridesmaid. Who is also her cousin," I whisper, horrified.

Megan hangs up and slides the phone back into her pocket. She walks along the part of the path that's dirt and not boardwalk, then takes a hard turn into the woods.

I squint. What's that? Someone else is in the woods! I can't see who — or what — but feel a distinct vibe.

Not just a bad vibe, but a decidedly ominous one. Eep.

"Oops, sorry," Megan says and runs off.

What was going on?

She's jogging down the boardwalk, on the other half of the loop, the one the rest of the group isn't on.

A few seconds later, she crumples Jessa's business card and throws it onto the wooden plank.

The vision faded and I was back standing on the boardwalk next to Oliver, the card in my sweaty fingers.

"Whoa," I whispered, handing him the card. Oliver quickly stuck it in his pocket, as if he wanted to get it away from me. My legs felt unsteady.

Oliver seemed to sense this because he slid his arm around my shoulders. "Are you okay?"

I nodded, still wobbly on my feet.

"Do you want to go home?"

Part of me wanted to say yes and burrow under the covers for the next couple of days. But this vision made me even more curious about what happened to Megan. "No. We need to find Tiffany."

"Okay. You should have some water before we go any further." He reached into his backpack.

As reluctant as I was to leave his embrace, I gratefully gulped down several mouthfuls.

"How's your head?" He asked while screwing on the bottle cap. "I know you've had headaches in the past after visions."

I rubbed my temple, where a faint throb lingered. "It's

somewhere between an annoying hangover and the start of PMS. I'll live. Let's go."

"Hang on." He rummaged around a side pocket and fished out a small bottle of Advil. He shook the bottle and the pills rattled. "Will these work? I stash these little bottles everywhere, because, you know, middle age."

"Give me two." I gulped the pain relievers down, figuring they might not take away the headache but could work wonders on my back. "Thanks. You're a lifesaver."

He reached for my hand again and we started to walk, quicker this time.

"Tell me what you saw."

I relayed the vision to him, describing in detail the shadow-shrouded figure in the woods. "It creeps me out to even remember it."

"Who could've been in the woods?" he mused aloud.

"I couldn't see because it happened so fast. It didn't feel..." I swallowed a lump of fear.

"Didn't feel like what?"

"A person," I murmured.

Oliver sucked in a breath. "Okay, let's put this conversation on hold. We're almost at the pond."

In the middle of the night, we were headed to a secluded pond where we hoped to contact Tiffany. But the deeper we went into the swamp, the more I questioned the wisdom of this late-night expedition. I couldn't shake the prickle of unease creeping up my spine. The ominous atmosphere clung to us like the humid air.

We powered down the path in silence while gripping each other's hands. I tried to focus on deep breathing, the kind one does in yoga class. That led me to thinking about yoga, and fitness, and exercise.

Maybe my mind was dissociating from the situation at

hand. Then again, what was the harm in that? Then a question formed.

"Wait," I said, pulling Oliver to a stop.

"What's wrong?"

"Nothing. A thought just came to me. If Megan's dead, maybe I can talk to her ghost." I let go of his hand. It seemed too intimate to look him straight in the face while touching his hand.

He bit his lip and considered this for a bit. "Not all dead people turn into ghosts, because not everyone who dies goes to the In Between."

That took a second to absorb. "Really? I was under the impression that if you were murdered, you'd go into limbo, er, the In Between."

He shook his head. "From my research, that's not the case. No one's figured out who goes to the In Between, or why. Of course, I can't communicate with the ghosts, so I don't have all the answers."

"Oh, dear. People arrive at the In Between randomly? There's no rhyme or reason?"

He nodded. Well, that complicated things. It also led me down a path of existential angst, which is exactly where I didn't want to travel at the age of forty-seven.

"But," Oliver said, putting his hands on my upper arms and squeezing gently, "Perhaps when you talk to these ghosts, we can start to take note of patterns and details, and try to figure it out. There has to be some common denominator with all the people who reside in the In Between."

I liked that he said *we*. I also liked his touch. I shivered a little, and not from the cool breeze or fear. His nearness was a little too wonderful given the circumstances, so I nodded, and beckoned for him to continue down the boardwalk.

"That's a plan," I said briskly, hoping the heat surging into my face wasn't about to turn into a hot flash. "Oh, and that reminds me of another question. If you can see ghosts, doesn't that mean *you* have paranormal powers?"

When I first arrived, Oliver had told me that unlike many in town, he didn't have any special psychic or paranormal abilities.

He chuckled softly. "Most people can see ghosts. They just don't open their minds enough for it to register. It's not really an ability or power."

"Whoa, that's deep."

Q and A was over, because by now, Oliver and I reached the sandy shore of the pond, our flashlights cutting through the darkness. The water was still and black as ink. I shined my light at the surface, half expecting to see Tiffany's ghostly form bobbing around.

But there was nothing except the glass-like surface.

I knelt by the water's edge, the sand cool and damp beneath my bare knees. "Tiffany? Hello?" My voice sounded small and timid in the darkness.

No answer. I felt a little foolish, talking to the water. I uttered her name again.

Zilch.

Had I imagined my conversation with her? Momentary panic seized me. How embarrassing would that be if I dragged Oliver all the way here, only to come up empty?

I steeled myself, then slowly reached out and trailed my fingertips through the cool water. At my touch, the water began to shimmer with ethereal blue light as though a sparkly current was moving beneath it. I snatched my hand back in surprise.

A mist rose from the pond, forming into the figure of a young woman. Tiffany grinned, her neon outfit glowing ethereally. It was like a Lisa Frank illustration come to life. "Hey you made it! Totally awesome!"

Sixteen

Tiffany waded out and I marveled at how no water clung to her colorful, ghostly form.

When she reached the shore, she did a little dance, her fluffy, crimped hair bouncing. I couldn't help but smile, despite the eeriness of the situation. There was something endearing about this perky phantom from another era.

Tonight, she wore neon green leggings and a matching headband. She appeared to be clad in an aerobic leotard in varying hues of neon blue. How did she change her outfits underwater?

I'd had a similar ensemble back in the day, and hoped past me looked as cute as she did.

"Did you bring the radio?"

"I did. Ah, I also brought a, er, friend. His name's Oliver. Can you see him?"

She shook her head. "You're the only one I can communicate with. Or see. Other ghosts might be different, but I'm only tuned into your ability. Or abilities."

Oliver, who was kneeling on the sand at the open backpack, looked up. "Can you ask her if she minds me being here while you two talk? I want to respect her privacy."

I relayed the question to my new ghost buddy.

"I don't care if he sticks around. But that's odd, a man asking for permission like that. Usually, guys just do whatever the heck they want."

There was a story behind the bitterness in her tone, I was sure of it. Now wasn't the time to pry, though.

"Men these days are a little more evolved than they were in the 80s. And some guys, like Oliver, are actually respectful. And kind. And..." I stopped myself, since Oliver was a couple of feet away and could hear me.

"And what? Who is this guy, anyway? He's not your husband."

How did she know that? "Oh, no, no, no." I held my hand up in a stop motion. "A friend. Just a friend. I'm not married."

Tiffany floated closer to me, her neon illumination washing over me. "I can sense things from the past just like you can, but I don't need to touch them. That's how I knew you weren't married."

Well, that was unsettling. How much did she know about me? "Oh yeah? What can you sense?"

She leaned in so her shimmery form was inches from my ear. "You have a crush on the guy who's here with you."

I stepped away. "We're not here to discuss my love life. We're here to give you the radio and get some information."

Oliver stood and handed me the little white cube. He cleared his throat, as if he was uncomfortable. It must be odd for him to only hear my side of the conversation.

My fingers skimmed the radio and found the familiar ON button.

"Check it out," I said to Tiffany.

The beginning notes of A-ha's Take on Me soared through the darkness.

"Oh my gosh, I can't even! This song is, like, so tubular, I haven't heard it in ages! It's bringing back some totally gnarly memories from prom."

She shimmied from foot to foot. "It makes me want to dance. C'mon."

Tiffany grabbed my hand, pulling me into an enthusiastic, if awkward, boogie. I passed the radio off to Oliver.

Though I felt silly at first, I soon found myself getting into it. The cheery synthpop seemed to transcend our surroundings, transporting us briefly back to a more carefree era.

One where I had no rhythm. Okay, that described me at forty-seven, too.

Duck it. Dancing with a ghost in the darkness? This was my life now.

Even Oliver tapped his foot and bobbed his head in time to the beat while grinning. I recalled his explanation of how DJ Ghostwave broadcast to the living and the dead, which is why we could all hear the music. "You've got some moves, Amelia," he said with a laugh.

The song faded out and an announcer's baritone filled the night air. "This is DJ Ghostwave coming at you live on 88.5, WBOO, the sounds of the spectral sphere. Shout out to my dead homies listening in the swamps of Cypress Grove tonight. And a special hello to Tiffany out at the pond. I've heard she loves New Wave tunes like this."

"Did he just dedicate that to me? Rad!" Tiffany snapped her fingers and swayed to the moody lyrics of "The Killing Moon." "I love New Order."

I looked to Oliver. "Could Calvin have picked a more appropriate tune?"

"Kinda spooky, huh? But I love this song." He swayed a little to the beat and snapped his fingers.

This was turning into American Bandstand. Or Soul Train. Or Solid Gold. He saw me watching and stopped.

"Okay, down to business." Laughing, Oliver turned the volume down.

"Tell us what you saw last night," I said.

Tiffany composed herself, though she continued to tap her foot to the music. "Okay, last night I floated up like I always do, to see what's going on, you know? It was pretty quiet but I could sense people coming toward the pond."

I relayed the information to Oliver.

"That was us, and our group," he murmured.

Tiffany continued. "I bobbed around in the water for a while. Sometimes I like to swim with one of the catfish in the pond, he's become a friend. We like to tease the frogs."

Don't comment on how weird that is. Don't go there. I blew a breath out of my mouth. "Then what happened?"

"I saw someone coming down the boardwalk on that side, then walk onto the beach and go over to that palm tree." She pointed, then floated through the air. She stopped and hovered exactly where Megan had been found dead and made a big gesture with her arms.

Oliver and I followed, with him carrying the radio, which was still softly playing 80s tunes.

Tiffany zipped around the tree a few times, leaving light streaks in her wake. "The person was under the tree, like this."

She sat on the ground with her back against the trunk. "I couldn't come ashore, and I stayed in the water, about twenty feet away. Didn't want to get too close because I sensed something was off about the person sitting against the tree."

"Wait." I stopped her just as The Psychedelic Furs' Love My Way came on the radio. Something about her story wasn't adding up. "How could you see her when you can't see my friend who's standing next to me? I thought you couldn't see most people?"

Tiffany stood and lifted her shoulders into a shrug. "I don't know. I usually can't see anyone unless they have psychometry, like you. Maybe this person had that ability? That's what I assumed, anyway. Because I couldn't see the person who came up next — but I could hear them. And see the result of what they did."

I shook my head, as if to clear the cobwebs. Nothing was making sense. "Who, or what, else did you see?"

"The first person was sitting against the tree and had a scarf on. I couldn't see their face, but I saw their clothing. Looked a little weird and bland, but I prefer color. It looked like a girl, or a woman." She held onto the palm tree trunk with her hand and spun around, then stopped and stared at me. "The second person, or entity, strangled the person sitting against the tree. I saw the scarf being pulled around the person's neck and the tree trunk. Something like this."

She pantomimed standing on one side of the tree and made a pulling motion, as if she was grabbing and yanking back.

"But you didn't see whoever strangled the person on the ground?" I walked around the tree, as if inspecting it for clues. I scuffed at the sand with my sneaker.

"Nope. It looked like an invisible human was pulling on the two ends of the scarf. Who knows? Maybe it was a ghost. Sometimes I can't see everyone in the In Between, depending on their abilities and powers. There are some malevolent spirits who are invisible."

"Well, that's unsettling," I mumbled.

"Ask her what she heard," Oliver chimed in.

I did, and Tiffany snapped her fingers.

"Oh, that's right! I did. I heard someone say, "you don't deserve him.""

"Someone? The person being strangled? Or the person doing the strangling?"

Tiffany shrugged. "That doesn't make sense, does it? Normally I can't hear people who don't have psychometry. It's confusing to me. Abiaka, the Seminole Indian guy in the pond, says that sometimes strong energy can filter through to us in the In Between, especially if a being has especially dark powers. That night, I can tell you that both... beings, or people, or whatever they were, had evil in them. Both were totally messed up. I've never felt that, as long as I've been here."

"In what way?"

"Dunno. It was just a feeling."

"A vibe," I whispered.

"Oh, you believe in those 70s hippie things like vibes?" she asked.

"Uh, yeah, sorta. I didn't used to. What happened after you saw the person strangled with the scarf?"

"I swam closer to get a better look, but it's not like I could help, since I wasn't summoned out of the water. The person against the tree was dead. That's when I confirmed it was a woman. Older than me, but not as old as you. No offense."

"None taken," I muttered. "What happened after that?"

The Cure's Just Like Heaven was on now, and Tiffany sang a few lines under her breath, then continued. She didn't have a bad voice at all.

"Then you showed up. I went back into the lake after that, since I figured you could help her better than I could. I hid in the water and watched, because I wanted to make sure the invisible being, or whoever strangled the woman, wasn't still around. Not like I could've done anything from the water.

That's what blows about being in the In Between. I can't do much of anything."

The idea of an invisible murderer was too creepy to contemplate.

"Would you mind if I chatted with my friend about this for a few minutes?" I asked.

"Not at all. I've got the radio to keep me company. This is the best night in a long time, listening to this." She waved her shimmery hand over the little device, which was set on a palm tree stump.

I pulled Oliver aside. We stood between the tree where Megan was killed and the water. I filled him in on what Tiffany had said.

"What do you think?" I asked. "What are we missing?"

"Other than the identity of the killer, nothing."

I made a face. "Thanks."

"Sorry. Couldn't resist." The corners of Oliver's mouth quirked up. "We've now got two mysterious people. Whoever Megan saw in the woods while she was on the phone with Ethan, and whoever killed her."

"Were they the same person?" I gnawed on my lip. "And what about the statement Tiffany heard? *'You don't deserve him.'* Considering Megan seemed to be having some sort of affair with the groom, that's pretty serious."

"Then that points to either Lauren, Bella, or Nia."

"Or Ethan."

Oliver wrinkled his nose, which made his dark glasses wiggle. "I don't think he could've gotten here in time, unless he was in his car already on his way here, but it didn't sound like that from what you heard in the vision."

I shook my head.

"And I'm sure the police will check Megan's phone, and

Ethan's, to see where the cell signal pings off the towers," Oliver said.

"True. Ethan doesn't fit the timeline. Nia does, though."

Absorbing this information — and trying to accept that a potential killer might be at my inn right now with Jimbo and Sage — I scanned the water and saw a ripple on the glasslike surface.

"What do you see?" Oliver turned around to follow my gaze.

"I wonder if that's another of the spirits?" I said, pointing.

He followed the direction of my arm. "I don't think so. See how there's almost a double glow? I think that's a gator's eyes."

"What?" I yelped. "Now you tell me there are gators?"

"They're more afraid of us than we are of them," he said, grinning. "Plus, the park rangers do a sweep of the beach every morning at dawn. I've heard that the gators in this area tend to stay away because of that."

"Okay, I draw the line at gators." I walked back over to Tiffany, shaking my head.

She was swaying to the song "Under the Milky Way" by The Church. I couldn't blame her — it had been a favorite of mine in the 80s, as well.

"Hey, I think we're going to take off. We don't have any more questions, at least not right now." Anxiety was beginning to mount at the possibility that Sage and Jimbo were in danger with the bridal party. Although if anyone could get themselves out of scrapes simply by their wits, charm, and dumb luck, it would be those two.

Tiffany's expression fell, and her shimmer seemed to dull. "Bummer. I'm loving this DJ. He's killer."

"I guess we could leave the radio here?" I looked down at the little device. "I could come back and collect it tomorrow morning. Maybe you can leave it somewhere hidden?"

We agreed that Tiffany would leave the radio hidden in a garbage bin, under the plastic bag. Smelly and gross, but our best bet for staying undetected for the next day or so. Apparently, the rangers didn't work on Sundays, so even if I didn't return until Monday, we'd be okay.

She thanked me again and again for the radio "When will you be back?"

"Soon. I promise."

"Do you think you could bring a magazine?"

"Maybe? What kind of magazine?" I aimed my flashlight at the water. In the distance, two glowing eyes stared back at me.

I fought back a shiver.

"Tiger Beat. I'd love to see who's popular now."

I shined the flashlight on Tiffany, who squinted. "Eww. Too bright."

"Sorry. Um, about Tiger Beat. That magazine's kaput."

She let out a huff of indignation. "Well, bring me anything similar. Bop, Teen Beat, Sassy."

A twinge of sadness hit me. All those old magazines that I'd loved as a teenager were long gone. Maybe People or Us would suffice. "I'll try to find something similar."

"Awesome!" I had to hand it to Tiffany. Despite her difficult circumstances, she was indefatigably upbeat.

We said our goodbyes and Oliver and I set out on the boardwalk. This time, we took the route that we'd come down the night of the haunted walk.

"That's weird," I said after we'd been walking at a fast clip for a few minutes.

"What?" he asked.

"It's not silent. You can hear the insects and the frogs now. We didn't hear them before. I wonder why."

"Just one more mystery in Cypress Grove," Oliver said softly, and took my hand.

Seventeen

Oliver and I strolled into the hotel to find Sage, Jimbo, Freddie, and all the guests in the parlor, watching a horror movie on a laptop perched precariously on a chair. Empty cookie platters and Mountain Dew cans were scattered around the room, which had been decorated by my aunt in a style best described as "Addams Family meets the Beverly Hillbillies."

I hadn't had time to redecorate this room yet and wasn't sure how I should tackle it.

The walls were painted black with gold accents, giving the room a dark, gothic feel. Heavy purple velvet curtains blocked out the sunlight, leaving the parlor dimly lit. An ornate candelabra hung from the ceiling, dripping with wax from long-burned candles.

The furniture was antique, with clawfoot chairs and velvet fainting couches. A large grandfather clock ticked away in the corner. The fireplace mantle was decorated with oddities like skulls and ravens and unidentified objects in jars.

But there was also a hint of tacky. My Aunt Shirley apparently had never met a leopard print she didn't love, if the loud rug on the floor was any indication. There was a cow skull mounted on the wall. Probably I should give that to Sage.

A large velvet painting of dogs playing poker hung above the sofa. The tables had lamp bases made from wagon wheels and whiskey bottles. A large, big-screen TV took up one wall but for some reason, no one was watching that.

Freddie was curled on Jimbo's lap.

I considered telling the group that the best pairing with cookies was a crisp chardonnay and not Mountain Dew, but it was way too late for logic.

"Hey you two, welcome back!" Sage called out. "We were just having an impromptu scary movie night. Hope you don't mind we dug into those cookies. They were mighty delicious. We ate almost everything."

Jimbo let out a satisfied belch. "Yup, Sage and I polished off that entire plate in the kitchen. Hit the spot after a long day."

Those were the cookies with the tincture. Why had they started with those? Though judging by the giggles coming from Lauren and Bella, something amusing must have transpired. Maybe Sage and Jimbo were discussing the perils of midlife after the Menopause Magic. That sure was hilarious.

"Don't worry, we saved you a few cookies," Jimbo added. "Uh, but we did dig into the cinnamon rolls. They were out of this world."

"Nice," Oliver said, grabbing a cookie.

I surveyed the guests. None of them, especially the angel-faced Nia, seemed like they were capable of strangling anyone. Still, I wasn't eager to spend the night under the same roof as any of them.

"How'd it go?" Sage asked.

"Not bad. We'll tell you about it later." Oliver spoke in between mouthfuls of pie.

"I guess this is our cue to head upstairs. Thanks for the movie and the snacks," Bella said, pulling Ethan to his feet.

I felt terrible for her, knowing that Ethan hadn't been faithful. A similar situation had happened with my ex-husband, only after fifteen years of marriage. I wasn't sure which would hurt more: being cheated on right before a wedding, or decades later.

It was all heartbreaking, and I didn't want to dwell on it. But it also gave me pause about my flirtation with Oliver. Did I really want to launch into a relationship again? Was I ready?

The four guests slowly collected their sweaters, phones, and blankets, muttering about the late hour and needing to turn in. They filed upstairs to their rooms, a procession of sleepy bachelorettes in silky pajamas and a brooding, scowling Ethan. He didn't say a word or look at me as he walked out.

Come to think of it, neither did Nia. There was something more there, I could practically feel it in the air.

Once they were out of the room, I began to gather the empty cans. From her seat on the sofa, Sage stretched and yawned loudly. "Whew doggie, I am beat. Feels like those cookies acted like a tranquilizer."

I shot Oliver a knowing look. Maybe the tincture was more of a sleep aid.

Jimbo let out a thunderous snore from his armchair. Apparently, the effects were fast-acting, and I was a bit jealous that they'd eaten all of the cookies. I'd give anything for a great night's sleep.

"We should discuss the case while those two are snoozing," I whispered to Oliver.

He nodded. "Good idea. Listen, I don't like the thought of you being alone here with potential killers under the same roof."

"Me either," Sage mumbled, half-asleep. "You two figure this thing out and let me know how I can help in the morning."

Her head lolled to the side as she slipped into slumber. Jimbo's snores provided an oddly comforting backdrop.

"I guess they're staying over tonight," Oliver said with a grin. "I probably should, too."

"Safety in numbers." I smiled back at him, comforted by the knowledge I wouldn't be alone. Though I hoped all the guests were harmless, after hearing Tiffany's account, I couldn't be certain.

One of Jimbo's loud snores roused Sage, who peeled her eyes open.

"Hey, I heard y'all talking. I definitely think we should stay. Those guests are something else. I don't know what's up between the bride and groom, but I'm getting a weird vibe from them."

"I'll be fine," I said.

Sage shook her head. "Jimbo and I can stay, along with Oliver. There's safety in numbers."

I lifted a shoulder into a shrug. "There are a couple of rooms upstairs. Or you can bunk down here.We have an air mattress." But if they slept in the living room, one on the sofa and one on the air mattress, where would Oliver and I sleep?

Upstairs, each in an empty guest room?

Together in a guest room?

Together in my aunt's room?

I wasn't quite ready for any of those scenarios.

"Jimbo and I can stay down here. We'll take your aunt's room. Is that okay?"

"Sure." Relief washed over me. It wasn't like I wanted to sleep in my aunt's bed, and it seemed like Sage and Jimbo weren't here to hook up. Nor did I want to think about it if they were.

"Hunh?" Jimbo stirred. "Did somebody just say my name?"

"Yeah, let's go to sleep, old man." She poked him in the ribs.

Oliver and I watched, slightly mystified, as they shuffled out of the room. We heard them drag open the bookcase in the library and enter the apartment. Freddie followed.

"Are they... together?" Oliver asked, a confused look on his face.

"I was about to ask you the same."

We both shrugged.

"Where should I bunk down?" he asked. "Maybe in an upstairs room?"

I winced, thinking of the noise I'd heard the other day in the hallway closet. "I don't know about that. I saw an air mattress in the storage room. Why don't you use that and stay down here? There's plenty of space in the living room, and I'll take the sofa."

"Sounds good," he said.

As we set everything up for Oliver, I realized that he probably did have affectionate feelings for me.

Why else would a middle-aged man willingly risk his back, neck, and dignity on an air mattress?

Eighteen

When I woke the next morning, the first thing I saw was Oliver.

He was still on the air mattress, but it had deflated enough that he was sunk down and lying flat on the floor to one side, the one closest to me. His body was curled into a fetal position, his expression painful, almost like he was wincing.

I felt terrible, and that was even before I spotted the impending disaster.

Freddie was perched on the other half of the air mattress, the side that had overinflated. He was staring down at Oliver's feet intently, and from the crouched pose and focused stare, I knew he wanted nothing more than to capture some toes between his razor-like claws.

I made a soft *pspsps* sound, hoping Freddie would hear me and desist his planned rampage. No luck. He glanced at me and immediately dismissed my pleas.

Oliver grunted, probably out of pain and discomfort, and shifted. His left foot moved an inch.

That sent a signal to Freddie's brain and he pounced,

attacking Oliver's black sock-clad foot. By the time I hauled myself off the sofa, Freddie hard wrapped his body around the foot, kicking with his back paws. Oliver had precisely done the wrong thing by shuffling his feet.

"Hey," I hissed, picking Freddie up by his midsection. My cat took one last swing at Oliver's feet. "Stop."

Oliver sucked in a breath when Freddie's claws made contact with his toes. "Oooof. Ow."

"Sorry," I whispered to him while holding Freddie under my arm. "You can move to the sofa if you want. I'm getting up."

"What time is it?" His voice was raspy.

I checked my watch. "Seven."

"Mmph. Did you say coffee?" He peeled one eye open.

"I didn't, but," I grinned. "Coming right up."

I hustled into the kitchen, feeling guilty that Oliver had a rotten night's sleep. I hoped the quality of my brew and the second tray of homemade cinnamon rolls would make up for it.

It took me about fifteen minutes to prepare the coffee. Because of yesterday's brew mishap, I dug out a French Press from a cabinet, then took the second tray of rolls out of the fridge.

The baking would come in a little while, because I didn't want to pop them in the oven right from the fridge. I also had to distract Freddie with an extra-large bowl of wet food because he seemed intent on returning to the living room. Probably to maul Oliver's feet.

By the time I returned with a mug of piping hot coffee, Oliver was on the sofa — and sound asleep, cocooned in a blanket. He looked adorable, and I felt more than a little sorry for him.

And grateful that he'd put his back at risk to sleep on an air mattress to protect me.

A little snore leaked out of his mouth. Grinning, I set the coffee on the table nearby and pulled a second blanket over his feet. Extra protection against Freddie.

Better yet, I'd ensconce Freddie in the small spare room that had been used as an office, where I kept his litter box. My aunt's apartment was miniscule, part of the reason I was dragging my feet on moving here. I took my coffee and phone to the porch.

The cool air and soft morning light gave the neighborhood a charming, cozy glow, and I exchanged waves with a woman jogging past on the sidewalk.

This was such a pleasant way to start the day. I imagined myself doing this every morning when I moved here for good.

I sipped my coffee and stared at the trees for a while, slowly waking up. Mornings weren't my best time. Eventually I checked my phone. There was a text from Marisol, the older medium who had helped me evict the ghost who used to live here at the inn.

> I'm hearing you're handling an interesting case. I'm sorry I'm not there.

The text was sent a half hour ago. I smiled as I read it. Marisol, who I'd learned was in her seventies, was a morning person. She also enjoyed a good mystery.

> The Cypress Grove gossip pipeline is fast!

> It sure is!

> How's New York and your high school sweetie?

Promising. He's as handsome and kind as I remember, and he's single.

Impressive. How are his teeth?

Pearly white and all there, thank goodness. What's going on with the murder?

Way to get right to the point, Marisol. I sighed and typed a quick summary.

I'm kind of at a standstill now. I don't know where else to look for answers.

Follow your instincts. Go outside and ground yourself. The earth will tell you what to do. Take off your shoes and walk around.

I grimaced. I was already outside.

This seemed like New Age woo. But of everyone I'd met in Cypress Grove, Marisol was the real deal. She had psychic powers beyond anyone I'd met. She was a mentor to young psychics, including Sage.

More than that, I trusted her implicitly because of her decades-long connection with my aunt. From what she'd told me, she and my aunt and a few older ladies around town were a tight-knit group. They traveled together on cruises, had a robust book club, and had investigated mysterious happenings in Cypress Grove.

Marisol hadn't shared the details of those cases. Before she left for New York, she said she'd tell me eventually, "when I was ready."

I'd accepted that was part of living here, that I'd learn secrets and details bit by bit, and not all at once.

If Marisol said to walk around barefoot and commune with the earth, it was certainly worth a try.

> I'll wander around the yard barefoot. Oh, I met someone interesting yesterday.

I sent a long text about the woman selling the menopause tincture at the festival, including a photo of my delicious cookies. The tincture hadn't seemed to make any difference with anyone.

But I had to hand it to myself, the crumb on those cookies was among the best I'd ever made. It was odd. My kitchen skills seemed to have improved since I'd arrived in Cypress Grove.

My baked goods seemed... tastier. I was confident enough in my abilities that if I was on something similar to the Great British Baking Show — but for cookies — I'd be in the final three contestants.

I baked the tincture into a cookie, intending to try it myself. The woman in the festival booth said psychic powers are often enhanced by the potions. But before I could eat any, Sage and Jimbo hoovered up everything.

She sent back three laughing emojis.

> I know the woman selling that stuff. A delightful person, but a little batty. Her Love Potion #5 is something powerful. She had a real scandal about a year ago, when she mixed up her liquids while bottling.
> Everyone at the old folks home downtown was supposed to get the Soothing Senior concoction in their banana pudding one Thanksgiving but they accidentally got the Love Potion. The stories that came out of that place! Goodness, those older folks got it ON...

Love Potion...Sage and Jimbo...

I clapped my hand over my mouth as I recalled grabbing two bottles. I'd also been sniffing the love stuff at the festival when I was distracted by the chief. Had I accidentally grabbed the wrong tincture when I went to purchase the pair? Had Leah mixed up the potions again?

Why else would Sage and Jimbo get so cozy so quickly?

> Oh dear. Well, I guess we'll see what happens. I'm going to walk barefoot somewhere. Talk soon, xo

I set my coffee on the porch rail and shoved the phone in my hoodie pocket while stepping out of my fuzzy pink slippers. I eyed the sidewalk. It seemed a little too dirty to stroll around barefoot.

Plus, I was new in town. I didn't want the neighbors to see me wandering barefoot on a Sunday. Then again, I wasn't sure if anyone would look twice, given the goings-on here. Plus, it was Florida. Most people wore flip flops everywhere, but I'd seen more than a few folks barefoot.

Gingerly, I stepped down the porch stairs and quickly made my way across the lush green lawn and into the backyard. A cool morning breeze rustled through the squat palm trees.

The backyard was a tropical oasis, with vibrant flowers blooming in every corner. Giant prehistoric-looking plants, with leaves as large as small blankets, ringed the perimeter.

While the inn and its rooms were unusual, and in some cases, gorgeous, the backyard was a showpiece. My aunt had gone above and beyond, with a lot of help from Jimbo, I'd heard. That reminded me. I needed to chat with Jimbo about upkeep back here. The plants, while gorgeous, looked like they were about to swallow the backyard from overgrowth.

A small stone path wound through patches of grass and up to a patio area, where four cushioned lounge chairs sat facing the house. Somehow, mosquitoes were scarce, and I had a sneaking suspicion that someone in town had used a spell to scare them away.

I started by walking on the path, the stone cool under my bare feet. Then I switched to the grass. I strolled in circles, thinking about Megan's murder. The sun began to beat down. Sweat formed on my neck and a hot flash loomed.

Shade. I needed shade. The stone path led into a wooded area. I hadn't gone back there yet, but Jimbo had said it was all the inn's property and could eventually be developed. He'd suggested a pool, but that seemed ambitious for my first year as the Crescent Moon's owner.

I returned to the path and went past the chairs, into the woods. The temperature dropped about five degrees, making me glad I was wearing a hoodie.

For a few steps, I tried to focus on my dilemma.

Who killed Megan?

But I stopped walking, breathing, and thinking when I heard the loud snap of a branch. I froze.

Squirrel? Bird? Otherworldly creature?

Anything was possible.

I took another step, wielding my cell phone like a brick. As if that would be a threat to an attacker. Another sound came into sharp focus.

The sound of a person sniffling.

I went deeper into the woods, searching for the source. I found it about twenty feet away, behind a fallen tree.

It was Nia. She was in yoga pants, a thin T-shirt, and flip flops. She sat hunched over on the tree stump, her body wracked with sobs. Fat tears rolled down her cheeks as she buried her face in her hands.

My mom instinct kicked in. I rushed over, my heart aching

for her. "Nia, what's wrong?" I asked gently, placing a hand on her shoulder. "Oh, honey."

She flinched at my touch, then looked up at me with swollen, red-rimmed eyes. "I'm sorry. It's just that," she choked out. "It's just...it's too much."

My brows furrowed with confusion. "Too much? What do you mean?"

Nia shook her head, a fresh wave of tears spilling down her face. She seemed unable to form words.

I squeezed her shoulder. "Take your time," I said softly.

Nia swallowed hard and took a few raggedy breaths, trying to collect herself. I stood patiently, rubbing her back, wishing I had a blanket or sweatshirt to throw around her shoulders.

The morning light was now filtering through the trees.

Finally, Nia spoke. "I have a secret. A big one. And I don't know what to do." She buried her face in her hands again, shoulders shaking.

I nodded slowly, my mind racing. A secret? Did it have to do with Megan's murder? I wanted to shake the truth out of Nia, but I knew I had to proceed cautiously.

"It's going to be okay," I murmured. She stood and I pulled her into a hug, letting her cry on my shoulder. There would be time for questions later. Right now, she just needed someone to listen.

She pulled away and wiped her nose with the back of her hand, looking like a toddler. She was so young, and that fact made this all the worse.

"It's about Megan," she finally said. "She was sleeping with Ethan."

This obviously didn't come as a shock, since I'd had the vision the night before. Still, I gasped as my hand flew to my throat. "Oh, dear."

It didn't feel right to tell Nia about what I'd seen on the

boardwalk. Although she and her friends had wanted a spooky bachelorette weekend, they didn't deserve to deal with real ghosts or real murder — or my fledgling psychic abilities.

"So does that mean you... he..."

"Killed her? No, Oh Em Gee. She was awful but she didn't deserve murder." That sent Nia into another round of sobs. "Do you think I'm a monster?"

"Of course not." I stood, helpless.

"I was with Ethan when Megan was killed," she said through her tears.

"What?" Who wasn't sleeping with Ethan? "Were you and he..."

"No! He's the last man I'd be with," she cried, her voice cutting through the forest sounds. "We met that night because I told him he needed to end it with Megan before the wedding or else I'd tell Bella."

"Oh, duck," I whispered. She'd basically blackmailed the guy. "Where did you meet? What happened?"

She looked at me funny and continued. "I told him to meet me at a hotel."

"A hotel? I thought he was in Miami on business."

"He was supposed to be, today, but then everything happened. We met at the one on the edge of town, the Roadside Manor Motel, a real scuzzy place. I knew he wouldn't meet me for coffee. He's never liked me, but I kind of led him on."

"Wait, I'm not following."

She glanced at me with a bit of sympathy, then spoke slow, as if she thought I had a difficult time grasping the English language. "I promised him certain things. The thought of an illicit hookup was enough to get him to lie to Bella and rent a room. Of course, I never planned on doing anything with him, but he was horny enough to change his plans."

"Eww." I didn't try to hide my disgust.

"Right? I went there and he immediately tried to put the moves on me. Had champagne, candles, a really gross hot tub in the room, the whole nine. Then I dropped the truth bomb on him. I had receipts and everything because I hacked into Megan's phone."

"Is that legal?"

"It wasn't really hacking. I got her passcode. I work in IT."

I wrinkled my nose. Logic was eluding one of us, and it wasn't me.

"He was shocked, of course, and begged me not to say anything. He promised to break it off with Megan, then I left. But, get this."

She held up her phone. "I recorded everything."

"Recorded what? You got Ethan on tape?"

"Tape?" She looked confused.

I cleared my throat. Occasionally I forgot that young people didn't refer to audio and video recordings as "tape."

"You recorded him?"

"Yeah, that's what I'm trying to tell you. Listen."

She tapped on the screen and Ethan's voice blared from her cell speaker.

"Fine. Fine. I'll break up with Megan. I'm not that into her anyway, we were merely messing around and having fun. You know I love Bella more than anything. I just have a hard time devoting myself physically to only one woman, you know? I'm not a one-woman kinda guy."

My face contorted in disgust.

"Right? He's a tool," Nia said.

"Can't argue there."

"After Ethan said all that, I left. Didn't want to be around him for one second more. That's when I got the stupid flat tire. That part of my story was true."

"You're sure Ethan didn't have time to kill Megan? I know

she called him that night." Too bad we didn't know the time of Megan's call to Ethan...

"How do you know she called him?" Nia's eyes widened.

"Ah, the cops told me," I lied.

She shook her head. "I looked at the clock in my car when I left, and it was 8:30. The hotel's about ten miles from the park, I saw the distance on my GPS."

"That definitely doesn't match the timeline. What's the problem?"

"I lied to the cops."

"Oh, no. That's bad." I pressed the heels of my hands into my eyes. "You need to visit Chief Wolf and set the record straight. Ethan might be a suspect. You might be a suspect. You didn't give the police the recording, did you?"

"No," she wailed. "I didn't want Bella finding out that Ethan was cheating on her, not after all this. Her bridesmaid cousin was murdered."

"And her bridesmaid cousin was sleeping with her fiancé. Don't you think she deserves to know that? And don't you think that's important information for the police? And for justice for Megan?"

Nia rolled her giant dark eyes. "I'm not sure Megan deserves justice. And Bella deserves to know, but maybe not this weekend. Bella doesn't need more complications now. Her family now wants her to postpone the wedding."

"Look, I can't argue with any of that, but you must come clean with the cops. It's really important."

"I know." She sniffled. "Ethan's such a loser, but I don't want Bella to be hurt even more. From the minute she met him, I didn't know what she saw in the guy. On their first date, he conveniently lost his wallet. And get this: he hates his mother. What kind of guy hates his mom?"

I sighed. "In every woman's life, there's a terrible man. Or two. Or three. Sometimes we marry them. Bella has the chance to not make that mistake. You can help her avoid that by telling the truth now. It'll be painful in the short term, but worth it."

For the first time since I walked up, Nia looked at me with something resembling admiration. "Wow. That's kind of mind blowing. You give great advice, you know that?"

I let out a bitter chuckle. If only my own daughter felt the same. "Occasionally, I do. C'mon. I know something that will help, even if it's just temporary."

"What's that?" At least her sobbing had stopped.

"Cinnamon rolls. Trust me on this."

Nineteen

Nia wanted a little more time alone so I returned inside. There, a small crowd had gathered in the parlor. I was surprised to find a companionable silence in the air.

Sage, Jimbo, Oliver, Bella, Ethan, and Lauren all looked sleepy and subdued as they sipped from inn-branded coffee mugs.

"Morning," I said with a genuine smile. The people staying under my roof were difficult, and in Ethan's case, a philandering jerk. But they probably weren't murderers. Knowing Nia and Ethan's story had made me feel a little better, but I had to account for the possibility that Nia was lying and had concocted an elaborate tale.

Still, I had one job this morning.

I clapped my hands together and pasted on a smile. "Who's ready for some breakfast?"

Today, no one protested or complained. Even Lauren looked up from her phone with something akin to interest.

Oliver offered to help me serve, and the two of us went into the kitchen. I noticed that he steered clear of Freddie, who was atop the blankets Oliver had left folded neatly on the sofa.

"How's your foot?" I asked while popping the rolls in the oven.

He laughed. "It's fine. Freddie didn't break the skin."

"Oh good. He means well." We exchanged grins.

"What would you like me to do?" Oliver asked. "I'm pretty good at bacon."

"I'll take you up on that." I dug around the fridge and handed him the bacon, then told him where the pans were.

We worked in happy silence for several long minutes, him frying bacon and me whipping up another batch of glaze for the rolls. It was almost surprising that we were so compatible in the kitchen, since the space was smaller than some walk-in closets.

"Orange juice?" he asked, as I started to juice some fresh fruit.

"I put it in the glaze. But I can squeeze you a glass if you'd like."

He shook his head. "I know I'm a native Floridian, but I hate pulp."

He made a yuck expression and I laughed.

When I was finished with the glaze, I set the timer on my watch so I wouldn't overbake the rolls. Then I left Oliver with the bacon and joined everyone in the parlor. The mood was still subdued. Given the traumatic events of the past couple of days, I couldn't blame them for being withdrawn.

I pasted on a bright smile. "Breakfast will be ready soon. In the meantime, there are still plenty of cookies left over from last night if anyone wants a snack."

Murmurs of "no, thanks" and head shakes rippled through the room. An awkward silence descended. I wracked my brain for a conversation starter that didn't involve murder, affairs, or the supernatural.

"So... anyone have fun plans for the day?" I asked with forced cheer.

More silence, punctuated by the ticking of the antique grandfather clock. Jimbo loudly slurped his coffee.

"I think we might go check out that succulent holiday wreath making workshop," Sage said.

"Ooh, nice. That sounds fun." I nodded at the others, as if to say, see, we do non murder things here in Cypress Grove.

Bella spoke up. "I think we're going to go shopping downtown. Maybe get lunch somewhere?" She looked to Ethan. "If that's okay with you."

"Of course, baby."

His use of a term of endearment made my skin crawl.

Lauren looked up from her phone, her eyes narrowed. "And me and Nia? What about us? Hey, where is she, anyway?"

"I'm right here." Nia walked in. "I was outside calling my folks."

"Downtown is an excellent idea," I said, wanting to deflect attention from Nia, whose eyes were still puffy and red. "There are so many cute boutiques and eateries on Main Street. I'm happy to make some recommendations if you'd like."

Privately, I hoped getting out of the inn for a while would lift their spirits. The heavy pall of sadness lingering over them was heartbreaking. Except Ethan. He could go kick rocks.

"That sounds lovely, thank you." Bella attempted a wan smile that didn't reach her eyes. I wondered if deep down, she knew about Ethan's philandering. Given my own history with a similar situation, I'd bet she did. I'd known right away that my husband was cheating — but it took me a year to finally admit it, and another year to act.

But that was in the past, at least for me.

We chatted idly about local shops until the timer on my watch went off. I excused myself to the kitchen, where Oliver was patting the grease off the bacon with paper towels.

"How's it going in there?" he asked.

"Oh, you know. The usual post-murder brunch awkwardness."

Oliver chuckled as we piled food on serving plates. Carrying stacks of plates, we went into the dining room and set everything up, buffet style. I told the group they could help themselves, and everyone seemed to perk up when the scent of warm cinnamon rolls hit their noses. Everyone plopped down at one end of the large table and began to eat.

Soon, quiet chewing replaced the silence. Nia slipped in and helped herself to a generous portion. Color returned to Bella's wan face as she devoured her third roll. Even Ethan unclenched his jaw long enough to take a few bites.

Within thirty minutes, the guests had chowed through everything and decided to head upstairs to change for their excursion downtown.

As I waved them off, a sense of relief washed over me. The inn suddenly seemed brighter and lighter without its troubled guests.

Sage, Jimbo, and Oliver also left, off to run errands and make succulent wreaths. I had to admit, I didn't anticipate that Jimbo was the succulent wreath type, but perhaps love was a powerful incentive.

I had a quiet moment to tidy up. As I was pressing START on the dishwasher, my cell rang. It was Liz.

"Good morning, friend!"

"Amelia! You're not going to believe this. I brought Chief Wolf some herbal tea blends, purely as a friendly gesture." I could practically hear her wink through the phone. "I went to the police station. Of course, I also hoped I'd get some tidbits about the murder."

"Uh-huh. And did he accept your 'gesture'?"

Liz scoffed. "As if. He mumbled and stammered and seemed weirdly awkward. I didn't get any juicy details at all. But I did discover something verrrry interesting." She drew out the last word for dramatic effect.

I leaned forward eagerly, nearly knocking over the vase of orchids Jimbo had left on the kitchen table. "What is it?"

For an unknown reason, Liz's voice dropped to a conspiratorial whisper. "I was reading the community bulletin board in the lobby of the police station, and there's a notice about a puppet show today at noon on the community center lawn."

"Um. Puppets?" My lips pulled back in an involuntary grimace. "What do puppets have to do with murder? I'm afraid to ask."

"Puppets! Get this: it's the same troupe we saw at the haunted trail the other night!"

I gasped. "No way! The park performers?"

"Yes! I'm thinking we should go to the show and try chatting with some of them afterward. Maybe they saw or heard something. If we bring cookies to share, they're more likely to open up."

"Liz, that's brilliant. You're a genius." I was already glancing at my cookie stash, wondering if I had enough.

Liz giggled. "I have my moments. What do you say? Want to be my date to the puppet show?"

"I'll be there with jangly bells on. And cookies. Meet you at the community center at noon."

After finalizing our plans, I unearthed a small picnic basket and lined it with a gingham cloth. I packaged the rest of my cookies into cellophane bundles tied with ribbons. Hopefully the treats would serve as the spoonful of sugar to help the informants open up.

It was already eleven-fifteen, so I changed into a breezy floral sundress and flats, perfect for an afternoon outing of sleuthing. Grabbing the basket and sunglasses, I set off on foot into downtown.

The puppet show was being held outdoors on the front lawn of the Cypress Grove Community Center, located a block off Main Street. Liz waved me over to a blanket she'd spread under a shady tree. We had a perfect view of the simple stage, which was a painted plywood backdrop of a medieval castle.

"Oooh, are those your cookies? They look amazing!" Liz made grabby hands until I relinquished the basket. She immediately fished one out and took a bite, sighing blissfully.

"Save some for the puppeteers."

"Delectable as always. If this innkeeping thing doesn't work out, you could open, I dunno, a cookie delivery service."

"Thanks." I grinned and helped myself to a snickerdoodle. I'd told Liz all about my previous business that I'd lovingly created and built in my former life in California — the same business that my ex had basically stolen from me. "Been there, done that."

Soon a hush fell over the crowd as the show began. The puppets were adorable, with knights, princesses, dragons, and trolls. The kids in the audience squealed and giggled throughout the story. Adults nodded along to the corny jokes and terrible medieval puns.

Liz and I enjoyed ourselves, getting swept up in the humorous tale. For a short while, I could forget about the ongoing murder mystery lurking in the back of my mind.

After the show finished, clapping and cheering erupted from the crowd. The puppeteers, dressed in medieval costumes, took their bows. As people began gathering their things, I turned to Liz.

"Should we go try to chat with them now?"

She nodded, already packing up the remains of the cookie basket. We made our way to the side of the plywood castle set where the puppeteers were packing up their equipment.

Liz stepped forward with a friendly smile. "Hi there! We just wanted to say how much we enjoyed the show."

The puppeteers turned to us in surprise, then broke into grateful grins when they saw me open the basket of cookies.

"Why thank you kindly!" said the woman who'd voiced the princess puppet. Up close, I recognized her as Jessa, the small vampire from the haunted trail. She was short, barely five feet tall. I felt like a giant next to her. Her unusually green eyes were the giveaway. Perhaps they were contacts.

"We do love putting on these shows for the local kiddos," she said while reaching for a cookie.

Soon we were chatting amiably with Jessa and two other puppeteers whose names I learned were Andrew and Bev. They snacked as Liz and I complimented the hilarious script and flawless comedic timing.

Finally, Liz gave me a subtle nod, signaling it was time to bring up the real reason we were here. I cleared my throat.

"We actually met a few of you previously, at the haunted swamp walk on Friday night," I began.

Jessa's eyes grew wide. "Oh yes, some of our troupe was doing a gig out there. That was the first time we ever had a ... problem."

The other two puppeteers murmured in agreement. I chose my next words carefully.

"It was certainly unfortunate, due to the tragic incident that occurred." I paused to gauge their reactions. "I don't know if you heard, but one of the women on the trail was found murdered."

Murmurs of sympathy met my announcement. The trio exchanged concerned looks.

"We heard. And the police interviewed us, of course," Bev said.

"Of course," Liz chimed in between bites.

"So awful," Andrew said, shaking his head.

"Do they know who did it?" Jessa asked.

Liz and I both shook our heads. "It's still a mystery at this point. But we were hoping you all could help give some insight into what you saw or heard that night. We're, ah, looking into the case ourselves."

I tried to flash Liz a warning glance, but she ignored me and none of the performers reacted. Apparently, no one in Cypress Grove cared if regular citizens conducted their own murder investigations.

The puppeteers thought carefully, then one by one insisted they'd neither seen nor heard anything unusual.

"We finished up our final performances and were starting back to the car when the girl, ah, woman, came up to us. She asked me for a cigarette," Jessa explained. That was Megan, the, uh, victim. Said she really didn't want to be part of the bachelorette weekend. She seemed like she was having a terrible time."

Jessa retold the exact scenario I'd witnessed in my vision. It was so odd to hear her describe everything in detail—but it reassured me that she wasn't lying.

Sometimes my psychometry was eerie and uncanny. The fact that I still didn't quite understand it, or why I had it, only made the power that much more mysterious.

"None of you happened to see anyone else, at any point, that night?" Liz asked.

Again, shakes of the head all around.

"Can't say as we did," Jessa said. "We all went back to our van, as a group."

"Did you see anyone drive in or out of the parking lot?"

They looked at each other and shook their heads. Something told me they were being truthful.

"When we left, we went to my house, where we all sang Monster Mash for a social media video. We told the chief about this, because I live close to the park and the timestamp on that video shows we weren't even in the park when the murder actually happened."

Nodding, I hid my disappointment as Liz wrapped up the conversation by thanking them again for speaking with us. Though it hadn't yielded any breakthroughs, crossing the puppeteers off the suspect list still felt productive.

Liz must've sensed my discouragement as we walked to the car. "Let's go get a drink and debrief," she suggested, linking her arm through mine.

Soon we were seated at a sidewalk table at Ice Ice Baby. The server brought out two frosty mason jars filled with maple bourbon lattes — no alcohol, though. I figured it was still a little early for that. A copy of the local newspaper sat on the table, and the server asked if she could toss it.

Liz said yes, but I put my hand over the paper, thinking there might be a story about Megan's murder somewhere inside. "No, you can leave it, thanks."

I shoved it to the part of the table we weren't using. We ran down the list of everything we'd learned and unlearned in the past twenty-four hours. Though we were no closer to solving the mystery, voicing the facts aloud helped clear my mind.

Liz tapped her chin thoughtfully. "It seems the puppeteers are likely a dead end. But I still have an inkling that Helena is involved somehow."

"Oh?" I raised an eyebrow, interested to hear her reasoning. "But why? It makes no sense. There's no indication she knew Megan at all."

"I know. But don't forget, she has some kind of past with Wolf. Plus, she's made her dislike for the Crescent Moon quite obvious. She's sketchy and I don't like her."

I nodded slowly. "True, but dislike is a far cry from murder."

"Unless she's completely unhinged," Liz countered. "You never know what people are capable of."

She had a point. I mulled this over. We checked the newspaper and read a story about Megan, but it only mentioned scant details of the case, all of which we already knew.

"Guess who said this quote: 'we encourage the public to call us with any tips and will be setting up a reward for information. Copy that?'" Liz read aloud.

"Let me guess: Chief Wolf."

We both cracked up.

"I think his use of those dispatcher terms is kind of endearing," she said, a dreamy look in her eye.

"I'd think someone has pants feelings." I cackled and threw my head back.

She curled her lip. "Did. *Did* have pants feelings. When I found out he went on a date with Helena, that witch — not a good witch, mind you — I was extremely disappointed. How could I ever be attracted to him after that, knowing he has terrible taste?"

We lingered over our coffee, enjoying the shade and people watching, while telling another round of bad date stories. As we chatted about these lighter topics, Liz's phone chimed with a text. She checked her cell.

"Uh oh. What's this?" She angled her phone screen so I

could see. "Ooh, it's Marisol. She wants us to look at an article online. She texted me a link."

I squinted. "I need reading glasses. Can't see that."

She dug around her purse while I moved the phone closer to my face.

"Here. I hate to see you look at the screen from an inch away." She handed me a pair of leopard-print reading glasses.

Donning them, I realized my up-close vision was crystal clear. "I need a pair of these," I muttered. "What am I looking at?"

"It's the local paper. The online edition."

Displayed on her news app was the photo of me with the identically-clad women at the festival. The headline read, 'Triplets!'

"That's silly. But it's a cute photo." I touched the soft, slightly saggy underside of my chin. "My skin doesn't look so terrible. And my hickey burn isn't showing so that's a plus."

"No, look at the comments."

Normally, I never read the comments. It was a policy I'd begun when I opened my cookie delivery service in California. Comments, reviews, and ratings were a minefield that could set me back several lifetimes emotionally.

I noted several supportive words from locals who'd met me or my aunt. But one anonymous post stood out.

Too bad she can't keep her guests safe. She should pay more attention to what's happening under her own roof and less time socializing

My hand clenched into a fist. "What the heck? Socializing? I was getting coffee! Who would write such a thing?"

Liz sucked her teeth. "It sounds like Helena, honestly. A lot of us were convinced she wrote nasty reviews on Yelp for the Haunted Hearth because she and Shawnda had words over the chicken salad."

I handed her back the phone. The chicken salad at the Haunted Hearth was not only incredible, but it was also world-famous. "She had a problem with Shawnda's chicken salad?"

"Said it needed eggs."

My eyes narrowed to slits. Helena was clearly disturbed. "No!"

She nodded. "Unfortunately, yes. But it could be anyone who commented. Keyboard warriors love to judge. I wouldn't worry about it, but Marisol thought you'd want to know."

I took a deep breath, trying not to let the cruel words get under my skin. I knew in my heart I'd done nothing wrong. "You're probably right. I shouldn't give it any more thought."

Since Liz had promised to relieve her shop clerk at the Astral Attic at three, we decided to say goodbye. I took the newspaper with me, stuffing it into the now-empty basket. I wanted to re-read the article on Megan later and share it with Oliver.

As I ambled back to the inn with the empty basket, I resolved not to let faceless, anonymous malice bring me down. I had bigger mysteries to unravel.

The fresh air and sunlight didn't lift my spirits. Something about Liz's dislike of Helena nagged at me. Liz didn't have a hateful bone in her body. Not only was she the pet-sitter for all of her neighbors, but she delivered magic ingredients to home-bound, elderly witches (it was like a local version of Meals on Wheels), and she never prodded people to leave her store if they strolled in two minutes before closing.

I thought back to when Helena climbed off the police ATV at the pond the other night. In retrospect, it was odd that she didn't seem more upset like the rest of us.

Her behavior had struck me as abrupt at the time, but I'd chalked it up to shock over the murder.

Now, I wasn't so sure. The more I considered Helena's actions, the more suspicious they seemed.

Something else was unusual, too.

Impulsively, I sent a text to Oliver.

> Any chance you can subtly poke around with Helena's guests? See if they can remember what Helena was wearing before and after the murder? Anything notable about Helena, or anyone else, might be a clue. She's the only one we haven't really investigated. I figure you'd have a better shot of strolling to her inn and chatting them up than I would.

I included a smiley face, hoping he'd be up for a bit of sleuthing. His reply came a minute later.

> Good idea! Will do.

On a hunch, I also texted Sage.

> If you get a chance, can you and Jimbo comb the edges of the parking lot at the boardwalk? Use any skills you might have. Look for clues. Let me know if you find anything odd. Discreetly :)

> You got it! We'll be slick as a whistle.

I had a good feeling we were finally zeroing in on something big. The clues were starting to point toward Helena being more involved than she claimed. But I needed more evidence before making any accusations — especially since it appeared that Helena and Chief Wolf were acquainted.

Replaying my interactions with both, I realized that I could trust neither.

With renewed determination, I marched up the front steps of the inn, ready to put together the pieces of this mystery once and for all. The truth was lurking somewhere nearby. I just had to find it.

I expected to feel the presence of the guests when I walked in, but the place was silent. Before I went into the apartment, I walked upstairs and knocked on Bella's door. Nothing. Same with the room Nia was in.

They weren't here. I eyed the closet as I breezed past. I thought I heard a soft *thunk*.

"Nope, don't have time for you today, Mr. Ghost Broom," I said aloud.

Freddie was thrilled to see me, and rubbed his face on my shins as I cleaned out the picnic basket. I extracted the newspaper, which was folded in quarters to the article on Megan and set it on the kitchen counter. A photo of her standing in a formal dress accompanied the story. It was clearly taken during better times; she looked younger, happier, and more relaxed.

I tilted my head. Jeez, in this photo she looked so much like... Liz.

"Oh, my goodness," I whispered, pressing my hands to my mouth in horror. "She looks like Liz and... Helena hates Liz."

Freddie answered me with a slightly judgmental *mmmrow* noise, as if to say, *yeah lady, I think you're finally using your two brain cells for once.*

My stomach clenched as I considered whether Helena was the killer. If she'd mistaken Megan for Liz, then perhaps she'd killed the wrong woman. Helena was slight, but if she practiced black magic like Liz claimed...

Helena could've strangled Megan with her scarf.

The phone chirping with a call startled me out of my thoughts. It was Sage.

"We found something interesting in a bag," she shouted. "We'll be right over as soon as Jimbo catches this python."

I froze.

"Amelia? You there?" Sage said.

"A python?" I asked weakly.

"Yeah, it's not supposed to be here. It's a non-native. Oh, wait. Jimbo needs help getting it in the truck. We'll be over soon." She hung up.

"What the duck?" I whispered, shaking my head. The snake was a distraction. *Stay focused.*

I paced the small apartment, trying to put the pieces together. My mind spun with possibilities. If only Sage had told me what they'd found. I had a glass of water. Then I switched to a glass of rosé.

The alcohol didn't calm my heartbeat one bit. I began to list every detail and every suspect on a pad of paper. Things were beginning to add up.

When my phone vibrated with a text, I lunged. It was Oliver.

> Chatted with the three guests at Helena's

His next message told me everything I needed to know, and exactly what I feared. My fingers flew across my cell screen as I replied to him.

> Can you come over? I'm going to need a lot of help for what I'm planning for tonight at the inn. Not a party, but the reveal of who killed Megan.

I scrunched my eyes shut, hoping Oliver wasn't busy on

this random Sunday night. The phone vibrated and I opened one eye, hoping he hadn't said no.

Be right over

I let out a long sigh of relief. Maybe we could pull this off.

Twenty

The evening descended upon us with a fast-moving storm that brought howling wind, pouring rain, and thunder. If ever there was a perfect evening for solving a murder mystery, this was it.

By nine p.m. sharp, everything was ready. I felt unusually put-together and stylish in a dress that Liz had encouraged me to buy at a local shop a week ago.

Instead of my usual, practical, and comfortable khaki capris and T-shirts, tonight I was in a flowy, gauzy, hippie-like long dress. It was tye-dyed red and white, which both complimented and clashed with my strawberry blonde hair. I also wore the pendant that my late aunt had intended to give me. The ruby stone sat around my neck, cool as an ice cube.

This cool accessory wasn't just gorgeous, but was useful, too: it staved off hot flashes. The entire vibe of the outfit made me feel powerful, and perhaps a little wild. Dramatic, main character energy. It was what I needed for this... thing I'd planned.

Or maybe that feeling was false bravado, entirely due to the fact that I was about to reveal a murderer. Something that I'd never done before, and frankly, never anticipated doing. It all felt very Victorian-era murder mystery, if the Victorians were in Florida and one member of the party was a cowgirl witch in silver boots.

Today, Sage wore a long, crocheted duster jacket over her T-shirt and denim skirt ensemble. With her flowy hair, she looked like a cross between Stevie Nicks and something out of Yellowstone. Jimbo followed her around like a puppy, complete with googly eyes.

She wasn't the only one looking sharp. Liz wore a beautiful blue linen dress with new, neon green Birkenstocks. A chunky, white quartz necklace pulled the outfit together and complimented her salt-and-pepper curls.

"Come in, come in. Hello, Chief Wolf, isn't it a beautiful evening?" Liz's smooth voice wafted into the dining room from the lobby.

"It sure is, it sure is. How are you today, Ms. Lopez?" His voice sounded low and rumbly. He asked Liz about her dog-sitting clients. All in a softer tone than when he talked with me. Weird.

I was pacing around the table, making sure everything was set. I'd put out a massive spread of food in the lobby, everything from leftover cinnamon rolls to cookies, deviled eggs, crudités, mini quiches, and pigs-in-blankets. I'd thought about cocktails, but decided that alcohol, combined with the subject matter, might not be a winning combination.

All of the focus needed to be on the case, and the details.

The murmurs of the guests' voices quickly grew to a more audible level. I went to the table at the front of the room and made sure I had what I needed. Laptop? Check. Power point done by Oliver? Check. Coffee? Check.

Enough courage to get through this? I wasn't certain of that. My neck was already sweating.

The door swung open. It was Oliver, holding a paper sack printed with the local bagel shop's logo. Only Liz and I knew what was inside, and it wasn't bagels. "I think we're set. Are you okay?"

I nodded. "Let's call everyone in."

One by one, they all filed inside, some carrying small plates of food. First, Bella, Ethan, Lauren, and Nia. They took seats along one side of the long table. Then, across from them: Helena and her three guests. Oliver sat off to the side, to my right.

A pirate sat on my left. I blinked at the young woman. Her eyes looked familiar, and then it clicked. "Oh, you're the performer. The vampire. The puppeteer. I almost didn't recognize you in the buccaneer getup."

"After the puppet show, I worked a shift at Long Prawn Silver's. Liz called and invited all of us who were in the park that night, but I was the only one who could come because everyone else has night jobs. These cookies are incredible, by the way."

She looked about twenty, with wide brown eyes and supple, perfectly unlined, deep brown skin. Poor kid, she had no idea what she was in for. Maybe she could use tonight as a character study for her acting.

Two more people swaggered in and took seats. Gregg the reporter, then Chief Christopher Wolf.

Gregg plopped down directly across from me, looking every bit as sweaty as when I saw him at the festival. Poor dude. But, who invited him? I didn't mind that he was here, however. If all went well, I'd clear my name — and having that information in the paper for all the town to see might not be a bad thing.

The Chief remained standing, in back of Gregg. He stared at me, hard. I didn't know how he'd take what I had to say, but this was the only way I'd feel comfortable unveiling my theories.

In public, with safety in numbers.

The Chief, I realized, might be compromised. Soon we'd find out.

Liz, Sage, and Jimbo walked in, and took seats against the wall. Feeling dramatic because of my long, flowy skirt, I stepped to the table and the computer. Part of me wished I could dramatically sweep everything off the table with my arm, then unroll a parchment map.

Instead, I smiled.

"Thank you all for coming here tonight, and at the last minute," I said. "I figured you'd all want to be here while we held a sage ritual and a blessing ceremony in Megan's memory. We've all gone through so much these past few days, and I feel like it's important for some closure."

The chief cleared his throat impatiently.

I couldn't let him throw me off with his stern attitude. It was almost time for my big reveal. Before I could say another word, though, the door opened. A curvy woman with a silver pixie cut and freckled, pale skin, stepped inside. She didn't look familiar, and I assumed she was looking for lodging.

Perfect timing.

"I'm so sorry, we're closed for the night," I said to her. "We're holding a meeting here—"

"I know. I came for that meeting. I'm local."

I paused, momentarily stunned into silence. Who was she? I looked helplessly to Liz, who was beaming. She rose from her seat and rounded the table to come stand next to me. She leaned in and whispered, "Don't worry. I know her. She'll explain everything later, and I'll fill in any other missing details. She's just going to observe."

"Oh." I glanced at the woman, who had taken a seat along

the wall near Jimbo and Sage. The woman was dressed in a classy black dress and black heels, making the rest of us look a little slobby.

It wasn't the weirdest thing that had happened in Cypress Grove, so I could roll with it.

I tried to ignore her as I spoke, but it was difficult. She had a commanding presence and flashing blue eyes. The mysterious woman seemed to be around my age, perhaps a few years older — and yet the intense focus on her face made her appear decades younger. She took in everyone at the table as if she were cataloging them.

"Before I continue, would anyone like to address the group?" I asked, momentarily off-kilter.

Sage raised her hand, and I pointed at her. "Yes?"

I expected this from Sage. I'd been to one of her full moon celebrations and knew she enjoyed giving incantations, spells, and rituals. She seemed to enjoy an audience, and figured she'd ease everyone into the evening with some inspirational words.

"You have the floor, Sage."

"Thanks, pal. Since you're all here, I thought I'd break the news to everyone. Man, I shouldn't say it that way, because it's good news. But I'm nervous." She tossed her long, blonde hair behind her and stuffed her hands in her pockets.

She paused as we all stared expectantly. A smile slowly crept on her face. "Jimbo and I are in a relationship."

It was as if everyone's jaw dropped on cue.

"I thought y'all should know. We've had 'em for a while, each had a crush on one another. This weekend we confessed. Feels good to finally get it all out in the open, doesn't it, Jimbo?"

He nodded. "It's nice to celebrate love instead of darkness, isn't it?"

The cookies! The tincture! The Love Potion #5!

Her words sank in, and I began to clap and nod. So did Oliver, and within a second, everyone was hooting and cheering. The two of them together made sense in a weird way. Even if it was the cookies that brought them together.

Florida man and a cowgirl-witch. "A love story for the ages," Liz said, her eyes glistening.

Jimbo stood and planted a smooch on Sage's temple.

She nodded bashfully. "Yeah, he makes my liver quiver."

I met Liz's eyes and she pointed at her midsection and mouthed, "LIVER?"

I had to turn away because I was going to dissolve into giddy, overtired hysterics.

While I let that image of a quivering liver sink in, I fiddled with the remote control for the computer. Ethan turned in his seat and shook Jimbo's hand. The mysterious woman sat with her twinkling eyes and small smile.

"Well, that's something special, something to celebrate," I said, slightly flustered. I wrung my hands. "And correct. Only light can cast out darkness. And I'd like to continue that theme today. Because the real reason I gathered everyone here is because I wanted to reveal who killed Megan."

Gasps rippled around the room.

"Amelia, I don't think this is appropriate. It's absurd, and I won't stand for you making a mockery of law enforcement." The chief stepped forward.

"No." Bella was on her feet, her eyes flashing. "I want to hear this. It's not like your department has given us any information on who killed our friend. Amelia seems smart. Let's listen to her. And if you don't let me, I'll contact my father, who's a state representative, and you'll be hearing from him."

Oh, duck. I sucked in a breath.

"I'll give you five minutes," Wolf growled at me, ignoring Bella. He tilted his head and pressed a walkie-talkie attached to his shirt. "This is Chief Wolf. I'm going to need backup at the Crescent Moon Inn. Copy?"

Static crackled through the little speaker. "Copy that, chief. Be there as soon as I can."

"Ten four," he said grimly, while fixing his hard stare on me.

I had to talk fast. The Chief was sure to arrest me for obstruction, or worse, if I didn't get to the point.

"Let's briefly discuss who didn't kill Megan," I started.

"I've got a PowerPoint here—"

"It's called a slide deck. Jeez. Get with modern times." Lauren sighed and crossed her arms.

"What. Ever," I muttered through gritted teeth, tapping on the laptop. The projector screen flickered to life. Oliver had spent the last two hours working on this presentation, and the first photo was a screen grab of a video.

It was the performers that night, mugging for the camera.

"Let's rule out the actors. None had motive for killing Megan. And once our group passed each skit, they walked back to the first stop, to the vampire. Her name is Jessa." I gestured to the young woman in the pirate outfit next to me. "The performers told me they all quickly joined together as a group, then took selfies and arranged their props, then returned to their van. During that time, they talked with Megan and Jessa gave her a cigarette. Then Megan left, and the performers did, too."

I tapped the remote, and a video of the troupe, singing the Monster Mash tune while in costume. "The performers immediately went to Jessa's home, which is near the park. Note the time and date. It's right around the same time the medical examiner thinks Megan was killed."

I clicked the remote. "Moving along. The other bridal party, the women staying at Helena's BnB. They didn't do it.

They were with Lauren and Bella for the entire walk, which also means it's not Lauren and Bella."

The women all smiled at each other. Each had an identical hue of teeth: blinding white.

"All five women, who don't know each other, agree they were together the entire time. They never passed Oliver and I on the boardwalk, and they wouldn't have had time to run around the other side, kill her, and run back."

A few people nodded. Good. I was making sense, at least.

"Now things get a little more complex," I said as we navigated to the next slide, with Nia's name and a question mark. "Nia. She came into Cypress Grove late, looking disheveled. Her shoes were muddy. But it wasn't her. It also wasn't Ethan."

A picture of a generic clip art of a man flashed on the screen.

"Ethan was a suspect in my mind. He arrived the next day, looking out of sorts and suspicious." I took a deep breath. In some ways, what I was about to say was as difficult as revealing the murderer — because everyone alive would be miserable. I angled my body so I could address one person directly.

"Bella, I'm not going to get into what transpired between Nia, Ethan, and Megan. Just know you have a dear and true friend in Nia, and don't ever forget that. Also, you might want to call off your wedding. Trust me on this. No one tells the truth like a middle aged, divorced woman who has zero ducks to give."

"Ducks?" someone murmured.

Bella's face drained of color. I chewed on my lip, feeling terribly for her. Nia leaned in and whispered something in her ear.

Bella then turned to Ethan. "You... you... prick!"

The sound of her palm hitting his cheek was loud and admittedly satisfying. And entirely warranted, as far as I was concerned. Bella jumped from her seat and ran from the room, followed closely by Lauren and Nia. Ethan remained, his eyes turning red.

"You must've had that coming, bro," Jessa the pirate said to Ethan.

Everyone ignored that.

"So, that leaves—"

Someone immediately cut in, interrupting my reveal.

"You and Oliver!" Ethan hollered.

I snorted. This wasn't the response I anticipated. "No, of course not. We found the body and had no reason to kill her. Why would I kill my own guest?"

"Liz." Helena piped up, her tone accusatory. "You haven't accounted for Liz Lopez yet. She's a definite suspect."

I turned to her with a tight smile. "I have not accounted for her, because Liz was at theater practice by..." I pointed to Liz.

She held up her phone. "Eight-ten p.m. Here's a photo of me at rehearsal. And more photos a half hour later."

"Exactly the time Megan was supposedly killed," I added. "She has a solid alibi."

"You can all see the time stamp on my Facebook page. It's set to public," Liz said.

"Boomers and their Facebook," muttered one of Helena's guests.

"Hey," Liz snapped. "I'm not a boomer. I'm Gen X. We're the feral generation. So, watch out, missy."

I held up a hand. "Okay, we can discuss that later. Liz does play a key role in this story, so please listen up. Helena, I haven't yet mentioned you. You're the only one who was in the park at that time who hasn't been accounted for. But I know what happened."

The chief took a step forward and rested his hands on the table, leaning in with a focused expression. Meanwhile, Gregg was next to him, scribbling in his notebook. Rivers of sweat had formed on his brow, making me wonder if I should turn down the air.

It was October, for duck's sake.

"Helena doesn't like Liz and didn't appreciate her presence at the swamp walk that night. She also didn't see Liz leave before the walk. She then mistook Megan for Liz — they were dressed alike, have almost the same curly hair, especially in the dark. They also have similar body types. Megan was wearing her hoodie up, however, and her face was somewhat obscured. When the walk got underway, Helena had her head buried in her phone. She did see Megan leave the group."

"So what?" Helena called out.

"Yeah, so what?" the chief asked.

Oh dear. This was what I was afraid of. The chief was compromised because of his relationship with Helena. I needed to speed this up and say a prayer to the universe that my evidence was enough.

"Helena left the group, telling one of her guests she had to use the restroom. I don't know if she intended to confront Liz (or who she thought was Liz). But she runs by the performers, who were gathered at a turnoff. Megan was with them, smoking a cigarette.

We suspect that Helena probably tried to use the bathroom at the visitor center, but it was locked. She went in the woods to do her business. Meanwhile, Megan — who was on the phone with Ethan and also looking for a bathroom — accidentally startled Helena and ran off."

No one in the room uttered a word. I took a sip of water and caught Oliver's gaze. He nodded, as if to say, *you're doing great. Keep going.*

"Now let's change perspectives a bit. If you look at Ethan's phone, I'm sure you'll find calls from Megan to his number that night. She phoned to tell him that she wanted to scare the other women, and she was going to play a prank on them by pretending to be dead at the pond. Isn't that right, Ethan?"

I shifted to look at him.

"I guess, yeah," he mumbled.

"Okay. She told Ethan — and he can obviously corroborate this — that she was going to pretend that she'd been strangled with a scarf. Which is exactly what she did. She set herself up by a tree and pretended to wrap a scarf around her neck and the trunk. All was going to plan, until Helena came up. In a fit of rage, mistaking Megan for Liz, she came up from behind and used her scarf to commit murder."

"You can't prove that" Helena yelled.

"Oh, but I can. When the night started, you were wearing black sneakers with frilly black ankle socks. When you came back to the beach, escorted by the police, you were wearing flip flops. Your guests also noticed."

"It's not a crime to change shoes," she said.

"No. But why did you throw them — and the scarf that Megan was wearing — into the woods? The bag was stuffed into a hollow tree trunk. We found it today, on the far end of the parking lot, far from the entrance to the trail. The sneakers have sand on them, just like the beach at the pond. We also found the scarf."

Oliver stood and held the bag up high.

The performer and Jimbo gasped loudly.

"My word!" Jimbo cried. "The smokin' gun! Er, the smokin' scarf."

I ignored him. "Here's what I don't get, Helena. Why did you hate Liz enough to kill her? And what did you mean when you said, 'you don't deserve him?'" I asked.

All heads swiveled in Helena's direction.

"How did you know I said that?"

I hadn't rehearsed this answer, but Liz piped up. "Amelia has powers. Far stronger than your dark magic. She knows things. She's more powerful than anyone in the room."

I couldn't help but notice that Liz then glanced at the unknown woman with the pixie cut, smiled, then added, "well, almost anyone."

"It was because of him," Helena screamed, pointing at the chief and making everyone jump in their seats.

"Chief Wolf?" cried Liz.

"Helena?" the chief said. He wasn't leaning in anymore. He was standing at his full, imposing height.

"Hunh?" I added, then immediately felt silly. "Wait, what? What does he have to do with this?"

"We went out to dinner. On a date," Helena began.

"It wasn't a date," Wolf said through gritted teeth. "It was dinner with a friend of a friend, for the love of Pete! I was getting to know the town. I do that with every new job. Copy that."

"I could even tolerate his little stupid verbal tic of the dispatcher lingo. Because, well, look at him." She waved her hand up and down his body, and we all gave him the once-over. He was an attractive older man, I had to give her that.

"We were getting along so well. Do you know how hard it is to find a man in this age bracket who has a job and teeth?" Helena shook her head.

Liz and I locked eyes, trying not to snicker. Helena wasn't wrong, but there was no need to murder someone over it.

"Fair," I said. "That still doesn't explain why you wanted to kill Liz and ended up killing Megan."

"Because Christopher asked about Liz! Because he spent our date, the entire night, talking about this enchanting beauty he'd met while in the dog park. She was dog sitting for a neighbor. Blah blah blah. Her hair. Her eyes. The way she petted his Siberian husky. Asked me if I knew her. Did I know her? She's my freaking nemesis! Who happens to be friends with my direct competition. And then I mistook Megan for Liz. Stupid. Stupid!"

She let out a swear word, smacking her palm hard against her forehead. I gaped at her, stunned that she'd just confessed.

"I didn't talk about Ms. Lopez the entire night, it was more like a half hour," the chef mumbled while staring at his feet.

He raised his gaze and snuck a glance at Liz, who was staring at him. They exchanged little waves from across the room.

The chief was obviously embarrassed, because his face was redder than a cherry tomato. Liz fought back a coy grin. This was an interesting development, and I couldn't wait to see what unfolded.

First, though, an arrest. Right? I looked to the chief, but he was still grinding his teeth and staring at Liz.

I didn't know if I should swoon, scowl, or laugh. Finally, I decided to play it straight, because an awkward silence had settled in the air.

"Uh, I'm not sure what to do now that I've revealed the killer and that Helena's admitted to the murder," I added, looking to Wolf. "Chief?"

"I'll take it from here," the chief said, snapping out of his big feelings.

I half expected Helena to try to flee, or at least put up a protest. Instead, she shook her head, stood, walked over to Wolf, and held her hands out.

"Go ahead. Handcuff me," she said. "There's no point in trying to deny anything now. I lost my mind that night."

"You allowed the darkness to take over," said the woman with the silver pixie cut. Her voice was rich and commanding.

After a weighty beat, the chief cleared his throat.

"I'll wait for my officers. Helena, sit in that chair against the wall and remember that anything you say can and will be held against you."

I wasn't entirely certain what should happen next, as I hadn't rehearsed this part. Fortunately, Liz held up her hand.

"Folks," she said. "We've got refreshments in the lobby if you'd like any on your way out. Including some coffee cake and cookies, feel free to take some home. Thank you for coming tonight."

Twenty-Two

Not exactly the best way to wrap up a murder investigation, but was there any correct protocol for that? At least Liz was moving everyone along. It was well past eleven, and most people probably had to work tomorrow.

Everyone but the chief and Helena filed out, talking quietly amongst themselves and sneaking looks at Helena, who was sitting in the corner with her face in her hands.

I approached the chief, who was standing guard near the door.

"Thanks for hearing me out," I said in a low voice. "I didn't think it would go down like this, though."

"Not a fan of the amateur investigation," he said. "But because it worked out, I'll let it stand. Why didn't you just come to the station and tell me everything?"

I exhaled a long breath. "Because I wasn't sure how close you were to Helena. I didn't want to risk the information being swept under the rug. I'm sorry I didn't trust you."

He nodded, a grim look on his face. "I understand. But don't do it again, you copy?"

"Copy that." I fought back a smile. "Anyway, I'm headed into the lobby. I'll send your officers in here when they arrive."

I left him and Helena alone, suspecting they had a few words to say to each other. Or perhaps not. Wolf didn't owe her anything, and she was facing the scales of justice.

In the lobby, folks milled around and munched from the snack table. I was going to ask Liz how she felt about the chief's obvious crush on her, but someone caught my eye.

The mysterious woman.

She was definitely a few years older than me, and I noticed her quiet elegance as she was sitting on a red velvet settee, slightly apart from the rest of the group. To my surprise, Freddie was on her lap. Because she was wearing a chic black shift dress, I knew his orange fur would get all over her.

She appeared to be talking to him in a low, soothing voice while stroking his back.

"Yes, yes, I understand," she murmured. "It's all going to be okay. I'll tell her."

Was she having a conversation with my cat? Like Freddie cared. She was his next mark for cat treats.

I rushed over. "I'm so sorry, I don't know who let him out. He's going to mess up your beautiful—"

My words and thoughts stopped abruptly. Now that I was next to her, I noticed the pendant around her neck.

It was the same as my own: a ruby stone on a silver chain.

"Where did you get that?" I demanded.

She stopped petting Freddie and let her hand linger on his back. "Get what?"

"Your necklace. Who are you? Why are you here? On today, of all days?"

Her smile was like a secret between the two of us. Except I wasn't in on it.

"I knew your aunt. She was a dear friend of our group, a mentor of sorts for our younger members. She received the pendant as an honored emeritus. The one you're wearing is hers. She wanted you to have it."

I blinked but didn't say anything.

"My name is Julia Torricelli. I'm the leader of the Circle of X, a coven here in town. We're the most powerful group of Generation X witches in the world, and we happen to be based here in Cypress Grove. I'm quite impressed with your abilities, Amelia."

My jaw dropped. "Uh..."

Way to make a great impression. But her statement took me by surprise.

"Well, thanks?" I said.

"I've heard how you've handled two spirits in town, and how you've used your powers for good, and not evil." She shook her head and gestured toward the room where Wolf and Helena were. "That one in there, she strayed from the proper path. Sad, because Helena had so much potential, but she embraced the darkness. She used to be a member of the coven. You, though, you've jumped in with both feet from the moment you arrived in town and you've pursued honesty and kindness."

That was one way of putting it. "You've been following me?"

She tipped her head back and laughed. "Oh, no. No, no, no. I'm too busy for that. I've heard from others. And I have my own powers of observation. Tonight, I wanted to see you in action. Loved every minute of it."

She winked.

"What the duck?" I whispered. "I mean, I'm sorry that my cat is ruining your dress."

"It's no problem at all. We were just chatting. He's a hand-some man, aren't you, Freddie?"

He looked up at her and squeezed his eyes shut for a millisecond. Was he communicating with her? I thought he only did that with me. Also, how did she know his name?

"So why are you here?"

"Amelia, I'd like you to join me for lunch sometime soon. Before she died, your aunt suggested I invite you to the coven but said it might take a few months for you to get settled in town and acquainted with your powers. I was going to try to meet up this month, but I'm traveling to Italy, then the holidays will be here, and you know how crazy those are with family and such. I'd like to chat before officially inviting you to the induction ceremony. I also have a task for you, just to make sure you're committed."

"Coven? Am I a witch?"

"Technically, yes. You're witch adjacent."

My eyes roamed the room. A task? I could only imagine the weirdness of that. "What kind of a task? I have a lot of ques-tions. What's required of being in a coven? Is there a member-ship fee? Is this like a sorority? Or the Junior League?"

Julia smiled. "It's a bit involved, and there are some physical clues. I'll explain more later."

This wasn't the strangest thing that had happened to me in Cypress Grove, not by a longshot. It was still one of many unusual moments since I'd arrived here.

"Sure. That would be fine, I suppose," I finally said.

Why not? I'd discovered that I had psychic powers, chatted with two ghosts, and solved two murders. What's a little coven action?

"Wonderful." She reached into her bag — an expensive-looking, minimalist leather tote — and extracted a matching leather planner. She unsnapped it and slid a pen out from an attached holder, then flipped a couple of pages. "How's... January 10? Oh, look, that's also Peculiar People Day. And a full moon."

"Appropriate."

The corners of her eyes crinkled as she grinned. Freddie chose this time to jump from her lap and make a beeline for Oliver, who held a plate of food in his hands. I swear, that cat begged like a dog.

"Don't you have, ah, coven business that day? Since there seems to be a lot going on with the moon and such?"

Again with the coy smile. "Generally, coven business happens at night. I'm just a regular, middle-aged woman during the day."

"Then the 10th it is."

"Haunted Hearth?" she asked.

At least I'd get the world's best chicken salad out of the deal. "Sounds good."

As she was writing in her planner, Sage walked by. "Hey, Julia. How's it going, cowgirl?"

Julia looked up and smiled warmly. "Hello, Sage."

I chewed on my cheek, wondering if she asked Julia here. When I saw Liz wave at her, and then Oliver do the same, I was convinced that one of them had something to do with this.

After she slipped her planner into her bag, she stood. I noticed she was wearing black high heels with red soles that looked suspiciously like Louboutins. "I will see you in a couple of weeks, Amelia. It was nice meeting you in person, finally. A true pleasure. I think we're going to do great things together."

I climbed to my feet, my lower back twinging with a hint of pain. There was a lot to ask Julia. Including whether my cat could communicate. But perhaps today wasn't the day to discover all the answers to all the questions.

"Nice meeting you."

"You too, Amelia. Excellent work today. You did good." She warmly squeezed my upper arm and walked out.

It was only then that I noticed that her dress didn't have a single piece of Freddie's fur on it. How was that possible? When he sat on me for any length of time, I came away looking like a sherbet-colored woolly mammoth, especially when I wore black.

I watched her strut out at the same time a gaggle of officers walked in. It was impossible not to notice that all the young, male officers checked her out, because she was that captivating and elegant. Like Jackie Onassis.

Oliver intercepted the officers and pointed at the closed dining room door.

Liz sidled up and handed me a plate. "I see you met Julia."

I scrutinized Liz's face. She had the most open, honest expression of anyone I knew, and I didn't detect any subtext.

Still, I asked, "Did you invite her?"

Liz shook her head, her salt-and-pepper curls bouncing. "Julia always knows when to show up."

"How... you know what? Nevermind. I don't need that information right now." I laughed softly.

"You feeling okay? That was pretty wild tonight, wasn't it? Can you believe Helena confessed like that?" Liz asked. "I'm personally glad Christopher wasn't into her."

"Oh, he's Christopher now." I bit into a cookie, chewed thoughtfully, then swallowed. "I'm a ducking good baker."

"That you are." She let out a chuckle. "And a pretty dang good investigator, too."

"What's up with you and the chief?" I asked, preferring to talk about Liz's love life and not the murderer in my dining room.

"Dunno. I guess we're going to find out. I will admit to an instant attraction at the dog park. Honestly, I thought he wasn't interested because the dog I was sitting tried to pee on his leg. I happened to have some Febreeze in my purse and squirted his pants."

"Aww, that's…weirdly romantic. I think?" I restrained a laugh because her expression was so earnest.

"After the Febreeze incident, I gave him some cookies I'd made that I'd stuffed in my bag. I'm not a baker like you, but that day I'd made some chocolate chip cookies. You know what's funny?"

"What?" I tried to tread lightly around Liz and her baking. Truth be told, it wasn't that great. I'd tried one of her cookies before and it was hard as a rock.

"You know that woman from Potion Commotion? Leah? She came into the store and gave me some samples. I put one into the cookie mix that morning. It was nothing magical, just some extra potent vanilla."

"Wait. Are you sure it was vanilla?" I tugged on my ear.

"It smelled like it. I guess." She tilted her head. "Why?"

I relayed what Marisol had told me about Leah and Potion Commotion. "Maybe you didn't actually give him vanilla. Hmm?"

"Oh my goodness," Liz whispered. "Do you think I accidentally made Chief Wolf fall in love with me because of my love-laced chocolate chip cookie?"

"From the way he looked at you, I'd say all signs point to yes."

"What if he's a werewolf? I hope the love potion stuff doesn't wear off too soon. Will the cookie bring that feral side of him out? Goodness, I hope so. Rawr." She made a clawing motion with her hand.

I lifted a shoulder into a shrug. "Does it matter? He's got a job and all his natural teeth."

We giggled in tandem, then quickly quieted when Wolf

himself emerged from the dining room. He spotted us — well, spotted Liz, and directed a smoldering stare her way. That was my cue to melt away and look for Freddie.

I found him in the apartment, snoozing on the sofa.

"Hey, little man."

His purr motor seemed extra revved up tonight. I stroked his soft fur and leaned over, resting my forehead on his back. This day felt like it had been three years long. The weekend had been a lifetime. This wouldn't be a bad spot to take a nap.

A catnap.

But, no. I still had to prepare breakfast for tomorrow and get ready for a couple from Michigan coming later in the week. They were friends of Marisol's and were in town to do a reading with her later in the week when she got home from New York. Come to think of it, I had to text her about the morning's events. She'd be thrilled to learn all the details of Helena's arrest.

Freddie shifted so he was on his back, paws in the air. I blew a raspberry on his expansive belly then grabbed his paw with my fingers and shook it.

"Can you talk to people? Hmm? Were you chatting with Julia? Why would you communicate with her and not me? I love you. I feed you. I give you tuna snacks."

A little *brrrrap* came out of his mouth, the sound reverberating through his entire body. I breathed in his cat scent, which was a mix of hay and clams.

It was entirely possible that someone, perhaps Julia, could communicate with cats. Of all the supernatural, paranormal, and psychic powers, it would have been the one I'd have picked.

"I'd love to hear what you really think of me," I said to Freddie. "Hmm? Would you be honest with me? Or would you be polite and not say whether you hate my cooking?"

The sound of a man clearing his throat made me look up. There was Oliver, in the doorway. He was holding a coffee mug branded with the Crescent Moon Inn logo.

"Sorry to interrupt," he said. "I can come back if you're in the middle of something."

I sat up, feeling a little foolish. "No, I..." Laughter burst out of me. "Don't be sorry. Come, sit. I was just talking to Freddie. Stupidly, I thought he could communicate with Julia. I guess I was hoping he'd say something profound."

Oliver's expression was thoughtful as he eased into a chair across from me. Probably he didn't want to get too close to a clearly unhinged woman who was expecting her cat to dispense a few words of wisdom on a Monday morning following a homicide arrest.

"It's true that some people in town can talk with animals. I'm not sure about Julia, though. I don't know her that well."

I shook my head. This place. "I was joking. Seriously, though, People can talk to animals? Who? Anyone I know?"

"Mostly a couple of the farmers on the edge of town, but there are folks scattered all over. You know that emu place near the interstate?"

I squinted. It was a sanctuary that also sold feathers in bulk from the birds when they molted. Witches around town used them in spells and rituals. "Yeah?"

"She can talk to the birds. The emus. Ostriches, too. Apparently she only can talk to birds that don't fly. She had a whole viral video with her communicating with the penguins at Sea World."

"It's going to take me a while to absorb that. That's... oddly specific." We exchanged grins. "How's everything out there?"

I gestured toward the door and the lobby.

"Well, Sage and Jimbo are holding hands and sitting on the

porch. It's weird. She hasn't had a boyfriend or girlfriend in a while. I didn't anticipate Jimbo would be the one, though."

"I didn't either. But good for them."

Oliver nodded thoughtfully. "Liz and the chief are drinking coffee together. The chief looks like a golden retriever around her. It's hilarious. And all of the bridal parties seem to have split, they wanted me to tell you that they're headed to Helena's inn to get the luggage of the women staying there. Then they're coming back here. They're also stopping at the liquor store."

"Great. It's going to be a long night."

"Oh, and Ethan pulled me aside, asking if I knew whether the strip club in the next town over was open at this hour. He's gone, thankfully."

"Ewww," I cried. The volume of my voice caused Freddie to give me a warning look. "Gross."

Oliver rolled his eyes and gave a rueful shake of his head. "Like I'd know what time the strip club opens. Jeez."

With most men, I'd assume he was lying. Something — perhaps it was my psychometry, or my female intuition — made me think he was telling the truth.

"Did the officers take Helena away? I couldn't bear to watch her being marched through the lobby in handcuffs and then out to the police car. It seemed too pathetic and sad, somehow."

He scrunched his mouth to one side. "It was pretty sad. But get this: I went into the dining room to grab something, right before Wolf and the officers took her out. The two of them were talking. Said she was so intent on killing what she thought was Liz — she called it a white-hot rage that overtook her, like a temporary insanity, her words not mine. Wolf didn't seem to believe her, though. It's going to be interesting to see how he handles Liz's quest to write a grimoire."

My jaw dropped and I pointed at Oliver. "Aha! That might explain why Julia told me Helena had 'strayed from the proper path.'" I made air quotes with my fingers. "Said she 'embraced the darkness.' Which I didn't think was a real thing outside of the movies, but apparently it is. Everything's news to me, though."

"There have been a lot of rumors about Helena and her black magic over the past few years, but I chose not to believe it. I try to find the best in people. I feel bad that I didn't pay attention." Oliver stared down at his mug, his expression sober. "Maybe I could've saved Megan somehow."

"Don't blame yourself. This is all on her. She chose to take the life of an innocent person." I did think it was the mark of maturity that he was being introspective. It was something I'd noticed about many men, heck, many middle-aged people in general. We tended to get fixed in our ways, never questioning whether we were doing the right things in life. Or treating people well. We assumed that because we'd been on this planet for fifty years, we knew it all.

Lately, I'd come to realize I knew nothing. And that was perfectly okay. Starting over wasn't so awful.

"Thanks." He flashed a grateful smile. "Listen, I was wondering. Would you like to grab dinner sometime this week, when things have died down? I know our last date, er, dinner, didn't go as planned. But I'd really love to take you to see this bluegrass band that's playing later in the week. The place has great fried catfish."

"I'd love that." I smiled at him, and as we stared at each other, it was as if the room itself pulsed with warm, pure happiness.

The sensation was so powerful, so joyful, that it brought tears to my eyes. But I didn't want Oliver to see that much emotion from me today, so I reached for a napkin. "I've got a mild cat allergy. But I ignore it because I adore Freddie."

Oliver nodded. Hopefully he was convinced, because it was time for me to ask him on *my* version of a date.

"But I had something else in mind for us, at least for tomorrow night. If you're free, that is."

Twenty-Three

Oliver and I stepped off the boardwalk and onto the sand. We were back at the pond, both hauling backpacks filled with towels, drinks, snacks, and tunes. The walk here had been the most pleasant yet, with frogs and cicadas and easy conversation as our soundtrack. The moon was half-full and lit our way, bathing the park in a cool silvery glow.

The storms of the previous night, both literal and metaphorical, had passed.

The pond rippled gently as we walked onto the beach, our footsteps making crunching noises against the sand. I inhaled the night air, gazing at the stars reflected on the dark water.

"Ready?" Oliver asked, setting down his backpack and pulling out an old boombox.

I nodded, slipping my pack off my shoulders. I knelt and rummaged through it, retrieving the mixtape DJ Ghostwave had made for us. It was packed with early 80s hits, and I hoped Tiffany would love the playlist. I handed the tape to Oliver, and the sound of the cassette sliding into the slot and the little door snapping shut sent prickles of long-buried memories through me.

All those little details of the 80s, things like cassettes and Aqua Net and Love's Baby Soft, all relegated to the trash heap of memory.

Oliver clicked play. The soft opening of Duran Duran's "Save a Prayer" drifted across the quiet beach.

"Can you hear that?" I asked him.

He nodded. "DJ Ghostwave said this is a magic cassette. The living and dead can hear it."

I wasn't sure how that worked and didn't need an explanation right now. I was too eager to see Tiffany.

After rolling up my jeans, I stood and waded into the water up to my knees, the small waves lapping at my bare legs. Probably I should've been worried about gators, but I figured my psychometry would save me. Or my new friend. Or dumb luck, which had gotten me pretty far in life.

"Tiffany?" I called out gently. "We're here."

I plunged my hand below the surface, focusing my energy. After a moment, I felt the now familiar chilly tingles rush up my arm. I swirled my hand in the water, and it left a spectrum of blue hues in its wake.

A ghostly hand found mine, clasping it tightly.

This was new. I gasped and pulled Tiffany out of the water with only a little effort.

Slowly she rose, the water slipping through her ethereal, bright rainbow form. Tonight, she wore dark overalls, a black lace long-sleeved top, short, slouchy boots, and at least a half-dozen necklaces. I was getting a distinctly early-80s Madonna vibe. I also wondered how Tiffany had access to such great outfits while living underwater.

Her permed dark hair was tamed with a bow, and she gave me a radiant smile.

"Greetings and salutations!" she said. "Thanks for coming back."

"Of course. I have a lot of news. And I brought my friend Oliver. He's setting up over there."

"You mean, your boyfriend?" she teased in a low voice.

"Whatever," I said with a smile. I led Tiffany over to the little spot Oliver had set up, complete with three towels spread out side-by-side.

He looked up. "Tell Tiffany hi."

I relayed the message, then gestured to the towels. "Here. Have a seat."

The two of us plunked down, and Oliver moved to his backpack. He cracked open a White Claw and handed it to me.

"It's the closest thing to a Bartles and Jaymes wine cooler that I could find," he said.

"Thanks." I held the can to Tiffany. "Can you…"

She shook her head. "That's one thing I don't mind. Never liked the taste of alcohol. But I don't need food or drink in my current state, so no biggie. But you should totally enjoy."

Oliver opened a second and we tapped cans. "Cheers."

As we drank, I recapped what I'd discovered about Megan's murder. Tiffany listened, rapt, as I told her what happened last night with Helena. She was especially tickled to find out the chief had a crush on Liz and that Freddie Purrcury was possibly talking to certain humans (but not me).

"That is like, bad to the bone. The killer was a dark witch, the chief is a boy toy for your friend, and your cat can communicate with some old lady. Gnarly!"

I opened and closed my mouth. "I guess that sums it up, yeah. It's quite… gnarly."

"And you brought me a second radio! Bitchin'! I put the first one in the garbage can like you suggested, and I think it's still there."

"This one has a cassette player, and DJ Ghostwave made you a special mix tape." I handed her the cassette case.

She studied it intently. Could she read his blocky handwriting in the dark? Who knows.

"This is a tubular playlist. I'm stoked. Tell him thanks, okay?" She looked up.

"We will." Mostly, I was just glad the music passed muster. For some reason, it was important that Tiffany thought I was at least somewhat cool. Silly, I know. But I genuinely liked the girl.

How she died, and why she was here, was still a mystery. But every puzzle didn't need to be solved at once.

"Space Age Love Song" by Flock of Seagulls came on and she clapped her hands, which sparked little twinkles of light all around her.

"Wicked," she squealed.

"Oh, man, I loved this tune," Oliver murmured while adjusting the bass on the boom box. When he was finished, he stretched out on the towel next to me. Tiffany was on my other side, on her back. She hovered about an inch off the ground.

"Me, too," I replied. "Saw them live one summer. We'd just moved to Kansas City."

"What?" Tiffany asked. I'd momentarily forgotten she couldn't hear Oliver's half of the conversation. It was so strange how she could listen to certain radios, but not living humans. Probably I'd never truly understand the In Between.

"This song. I loved it and so did Oliver. I haven't heard it in years." I explained that I'd seen the band in 1990 and how they'd played the song. As I talked about the show, I felt old as dirt. That had been a different lifetime ago.

"I was fifteen when it came out," she said, her voice wistful. "The first time I heard it, I was at homecoming. Rob Blanchard asked me to dance. He was the cutest guy in school. He looked like a member of Bon Jovi, you know, with the hair."

"I knew a few Rob Blanchards in my day, too."

Tiffany hummed. "It's kind of a difficult song to dance to, though, because you're not sure if you want to slow dance or fast dance. And if you slow dance to a song that's really a fast dance song, everyone in school thinks you totally want to make out with the guy you're dancing with."

"Yeah, I recall that dilemma," I said.

The first time I'd heard the song was on the radio. We were living in Oregon at the time, which was the place my family had lived before Kansas City. My brother Mike was driving us to school — the first day, in September, I recall — and for the rest of the day, it echoed in my brain. The lyrics and ethereal synthesizer were like an ultra-cool portal into another world, one of grownups and endless good times. Of clubs and parties and limitless possibilities.

Little did I know that adulthood was nothing of the sort. If anything, possibilities slammed shut like doors during a marital fight with each passing year.

Or, perhaps not. Life had been quite different lately, ever since I'd moved to Cypress Grove. I had so much to look forward to. So much to be excited about.

Growing the Crescent Moon's business. Getting to know my new group of friends, which now included a teenage ghost named Tiffany. Learning to manage my psychometry, perhaps with the help of Julia. Joining a coven.

Who knew I'd contemplate joining a coven? In the dark, I grinned wide.

Oliver.

I slid my hand onto the cool sand in between my towel and Oliver's. Before I could feel his touch, I felt the warmth of his hand over mine. Then the weight of his palm and the way he gently twined his fingers into mine.

Music floated through the cool night air. Tiffany sang along, softly.

"You have a good voice," I said to her.

"Thanks. I love to sing. Sometimes I just float around and look at the stars and sing and sing."

I thought back to that long ago fall when I first heard this Flock of Seagulls song, dreaming of the future and all it might bring.

Now here I was, years later, in a place I never could have imagined. With people — and spirits — that were like something out of a movie. Yet in so many ways, being here, feeling all the things, reminded me of that young, carefree girl I used to be, excited by new possibilities.

The future was something to look forward to, not dread. For once.

I gave Oliver's hand a gentle squeeze. He squeezed back. Before I came here, I'd been knocked around by life. Humbled by motherhood. Defeated by divorce.

But so much still lay ahead. Midlife wasn't the end, not at all.

I would continue my story under this vast expanse of stars, here in Cypress Grove, Florida. As I gazed up at the glittering, wide open sky, I felt something I hadn't in a very long time.

Hope.

THE END

---

*Thank you for reading **I WANT YOUR HEX!** Your support*

means more to me than you know. I appreciate each and every one of my readers!

***EVERY HEX YOU TAKE**, book three in the Crescent Moon Series, is next. It's available on Amazon, or request it at your local library or bookstore today!*

Gemma Hilliard's Pretzel Surprise Cookies

This is the recipe engraved on Gemma Hilliard's tombstone, discovered by Amelia during a visit to the Enchanted Eternity Park. Amelia was so taken with the cookies that she asked around town about the recipe's creator.

Here's what Shawnda Hersey, the owner of the Haunted Hearth, told Amelia.

Gemma Hilliard was born in 1942 in Cypress Grove. Though she lived a simple life as a seamstress, Gemma had a remarkable gift: she was clairvoyant. Locals say Gemma always knew just when to bake up a fresh batch of her signature Pretzel Surprise Cookies to share with neighbors, perfectly timed with their visits. Her cookies became the talk of the town.

For every holiday and special occasion, Gemma could be counted on to show up with a tray of her addictive treats. She never revealed the recipe, keeping it a closely guarded secret. When Gemma passed away in 2001, she had one final request: for everyone to enjoy her famous cookies in the years to come.

Each bite contains bursts of peanut butter, chocolate chips, pretzels, and cherries - Gemma's special blend of flavors. Even in death, Gemma wanted to keep sharing her gift of cookies with the world. Now thanks to her tombstone recipe, you can experience the wonders of Gemma's Pretzel Surprise Cookies for yourself.

Ingredients

2 sticks (1 cup) salted butter, softened to room temperature.

1/2 cup maple syrup

1/2 cup creamy peanut butter

1 large egg

1 tablespoon vanilla extract

1 3/4 - 2 cups almond flour

1 1/2 cups old-fashioned oats

1 teaspoon baking soda

1/2 teaspoon kosher salt

1 cup semi-sweet or dark chocolate chips

1 cup mini salted pretzels, broken into pieces.

1/3 cup dried cherries

Flaky sea salt for sprinkling (optional)

Instructions

Gather Your Ingredients: Like a clairvoyant glimpsing the future, gather all the tasty components for these magical cookies. Gemma felt an organized mise en place was essential. Don't forget to preheat the oven to 350 degrees.

Blend the Wet Goods: In a mixing bowl, blend the softened butter and maple syrup together like swirling visions in a crystal ball. Cream them until perfectly combined. Then add the peanut butter and mix until the flavors harmonize.

Crack the Egg of Insight: Break the egg into the bowl. Mix it along with the vanilla into the cookie dough.

Stir in the Dry Mixture: In a separate bowl, mix the almond flour, oats, baking soda and salt. The dry ingredients that provide structure, like the body houses our spirit. Slowly incorporate these into the wet mixture.

Fold in the Surprises: Now comes the fun part! Fold in those chocolate chips, pretzels, and dried cherries. These are the surprise revelations, like a clairvoyant seeing the future unfold.

Shape the Dough: Form the dough into rounded cookie shapes on a baking sheet.

Shake and Bake: Add a sprinkle of flaky sea salt, if desired. Bake at 350°F for 10-12 minutes, just until the edges are lightly browned.

Cool and Enjoy: Allow the cookies to cool, letting the delicious aroma waft through the air. Enjoy these clairvoyant treats with a hot cup of tea or coffee. As you take the first bite, embrace the gift of flavors and give thanks to Gemma, who foresaw the joy to all who experience her magical Pretzel Surprise Cookies.

Acknowledgments

Success is one percent luck, two percent talent, twenty percent having a good team, and seventy-seven percent never giving up.

To me, the most important of those is the team, and I have an amazing one.

Thank you to Rachel, Perrin, and Ashley at The Author Buddy. Your careful attention and editing of my work is so appreciated.

Also a huge thanks to Lou Harper at Cover Affairs. Your illustrations are perfection.

And, as always, all of my love to my husband Marco, who has been there every step of the way.

Tara Lush is a Florida-based author and journalist. She's an RWA Rita finalist, an Amtrak writing fellow and the winner of the George C. Polk award for environmental journalism.

Previously, she was a reporter with The Associated Press in Florida, covering crime, alligators, natural disasters and politics.

Tara is a fan of vintage pulp fiction book covers, Sinatra-era jazz, 1980s fashion, tropical chill, kombucha, gin, tonic, seashells, iPhones, Art Deco, telenovelas, street art, coconut anything, strong coffee and newspapers. She lives on the Gulf Coast with her husband and two dogs.

Click HERE to sign up for Tara's newsletter.

Also by Tara Lush

CRESCENT MOON MYSTERIES

Eat, Pray, Hex

I Want Your Hex

Every Hex You Take (coming June 2024)

THE COFFEE LOVER'S MYSTERY SERIES

Grounds for Murder

Cold Brew Corpse

Live and Let Grind

A Bean to Die For

Give Me Chills

THIS SERIES IS ALSO AVAILABLE IN HARDCOVER AND AUDIO.

THE CRITTERS AND CRIMINALS SERIES

Gator Queen (coming March 2024)